TRIBULATION OF A GHETTO KID III:

THE STREET BIBLE

THE GHOST

RICHMOND, VA

TRIBULATION OF A GHETTO KID III: The Street Bible

For distribution information and bulk ordering:
Web/Againstalloddzproductions.org
Email/whoistheghost1@yahoo.com

Published by
Against All Oddz Publications, LLC
 P.O. BOX 36297
North Chesterfield Virginia 23235
Interior design and layout by: Against All Oddz Publications

Thirteenth Amendment to the Constitution

Neither slavery nor involuntary servitude, except as a punishment for crime whereof the party shall have been duly convicted, shall exist within the United States, or any place subject to their jurisdiction

The fame is not my aim, greater there is in you
if you only knew...

CHAPTER 1

Just 24 hours after the U Heights massacre, the streets of Richmond were full of gossip about the showdown in Charlottesville. Some mourned and poured out liquor for the loss of some of the most respected street dudes ever to come out of the city. Among his peers, LA was labeled a soldier for the way he fired off on the police. If the youth could have their say, all cops did was ride through the ghettos and run down on struggling black youth.

For street cats, the four officers gunned down by LA were just getting a taste of their own medicine. It was like cops had a license to shoot young blacks down in the streets. But when roles reversed and the uniforms began to receive hot lead from the hate, that hate produced, suddenly all hell breaks loose. Everyone who knew LA was taken by surprise upon hearing about the vicious attack on the SWAT team members. He was a ghetto celebrity and those who knew him understood his aggression. He was pushed to the point of no return; *he'd lost it.*

Society would probably brand him a menace for what he did, not even taking into account the circumstances surrounding the tragedy. It seemed as though nobody recognized the struggle; all they saw were the troubles. A man could only take but so much before he exploded. And killing Bernard was like a major orgasm for him. After Angie's death, he lived and breathed for the day they would finally meet face to face. In a way, the two were bonded together. It was destiny that they clashed. LA didn't give a damn what happen after his meeting with Bernard.

After a silent, hour long trip home, Jeffery plopped down on his sofa and counted his blessings. However, despite all he'd been through over in Charlottesville, the night was far from finished. He laid back, listening to Dana's Land Cruiser pull off and trail down the block, and couldn't help but feel pity for the girl. Her love for his man, LA was more than evident.

Jeffery paged Tiffany, put in the code then relaxed, thinking back on how the night had unfolded. No sooner had he taken his first snore, he was awakened by the shaking of his arm, followed by the beautiful sight of his girlfriend. Tiffany slipped off her Polo sandals and jumped on the chair, straddling the youngster as she leaned forward to kiss him. Jeffery gave her a quick peck on the lips.

"Shorty hold up, we gotta go take care of something right quick." Tiffany frowns, but get herself together as he goes to retrieve his house keys. In less than a minute, the two are headed out the door to Tiffany's ride. When Jeffery approached Diane's doorstep at three in the morning, he took a deep breath, knowing this would be the hardest thing he'd ever done. No matter how it was phrased, there was simply no easy way to tell a mother her only child had just been gunned down in the streets. His heart thumped as he waited for her to come to the door. He hated waking her out of her sleep, but he felt it was only right that she hear it from him instead of someone else, or even worse, see it on the news. Jeffery just figured his friend would want it this way. Hearing her unlock the door and take the chain off, he nervously glances back at Tiffany sitting in the car.

Diane knew Jeffrey's presence there at such an hour meant trouble. She had dreamed about it and dreaded this day for years, and now like some *horrible fucking prophecy,* it was here!' She stared at Jeffrey with this terrible fear in her eyes as her heart pounded! "What is it? Oh God, something happened to Lamont...." She held her breath.

"Can I come in? Mrs. Diane... Please," he begged. Draped in only a nightgown, she stood aside while Jeffery walked past. As they took a seat in the living room, Jeffery's mind searched to find the most comforting words. Without success, he gazed into her pain filled eyes, regretting ever coming over there.

"He's dead Mrs. Diane... I'm so sorry." A single tear falls from his eye as the words coming from his own mouth stings him.

"Lord... Oh God, nooo Jeffrey!!" She moaned. "Jeffery, baby... Please don-," she grips her chest as if she's about to have a heart attack. He knew that she had very bad asthma, so he quickly asked if there was something that he could do to help. She gasped for air, apparently losing her breath. Barely able to talk, she managed to utter out something about a purse, which was in the other room. Jeffery vanished to the direction she was pointing in. He was back in a flash with her purse. She snatched it from his hand, ransacking through it, and tossing things to the side until she found what she was looking for.

While Diane sucked on the inhaler, Jeffery disappeared into the kitchen as the asthma medication did its job. She was breathing normally by the time he returned with a cold glass of water. She put the pump on the coffee table and breaks out in tears.

"Lord, you killing me! I can't take no more!" She shouts and slams her fist down repeatedly on the table in front of her. Jeffery quickly takes hold of her before she injured herself.

"Jeffery, what happened to my baby?" The poor woman cried out so loud Tiffany heard the commotion from outside in the car. When she entered the house, Diane was crying profusely, while Jeffery restrained her movements. Tiffany couldn't help but feel compassion for the lady. She rushed by Jeffrey's side to assist him in comforting the hysterical woman as she relieved her motherly grief. They stayed with her until she finally calmed down. As the pair was leaving the house, Jeffrey turned to her and offered his condolences.

"Mrs. Diane, again I'm sorry, but I'd rather you get the news from me than the cops." She was indeed grateful for Jeffrey coming by. Besides, it wasn't like she didn't see it coming. The detective warned her about this day. If only she would have listened.

The Ghost

CHAPTER 2

Almost two months had passed since Black had shaved or cut his hair. At a glance, he could easily be mistaken for a Neanderthal. Although his facial appearance wasn't up to par, he'd managed to keep his body structure intact by doing a minimum of five hundred push ups a day. He even shadowboxed from time to time. Black danced around in the tiny cell, throwing swift punches while trash talking, as if he were fighting an imaginary opponent. The boy looked pretty too. The way he moved his feet and slugged combinations at the air was nothing short of professional.

On Tuesdays and Thursdays, the deputy came around with the trustee, passing out clean underwear and linen. Because Black knew the old cat, Doc from the streets, he got to change his stuff every other day. He was relieved to hear the laundry cot rolling down the hall. The guards yelled for all inmates to throw out their dirty linen in exchange for clean ones. Showers were only three times a week and Black looked forward to taking his. Missing it would mean he'd have to wait three more days until Friday.

As he stood there in the cell, wiping the sweat from his soaked body with a towel, he heard a single knock at the door. When he peeked out, no one was there.

"**Strange**," Black thought and turned and started to walk to his bunk when he notices what appeared to be an envelope with a note inside laying on the floor. Puzzled, he quickly picked it up and smiled when he felt the three cigarettes inside, realizing they'd come from Doc. Upon opening it, there was a note inside. He sat down on the steel toilet and unfolded the piece of paper. It read.

Black,

I hate to lay this shit on you man. It's about your stick man LA. Police killed him youngster!!! It was a big shootout somewhere in Charlottesville. 9 motherfuckers got killed!! Shit is all over the news my nigga, they even had his face on TV. Your man snapped. They said he killed a white dude in North Carolina. Oh, the cat you was telling me about, Bernard. Yeah, they say your man killed him and then shot up four cops. Like I say man, I hate to bring you bad news but I gotta give it to him. The nigga went out gunning like a real nigga suppose too. Need anything, holla.

"Can't be," Black stared frantically around the cell. "Please God, don't let this be true. Don't do this shit to me!" Panic settling in, he jumps up and hugs the bars and began yelling out, "Deputyyy! Yo Deputyyyy!"

Angry tears streams from his eyes. He tried to shake the bars to no avail. The angrier he got, the more he started to look like something from Wild Kingdom.

"**Motherfuckers**!" Tired of hollering, he sat down on his bunk. "My nigga can't be dead," he kept repeating to himself.

The sound of keys brought him back to his feet. "I gotta make a call," he yelled to the chubby, African American deputy approaching his cell.

"Johnson, what the hell you banging for?"

"I got some issues Dept. Please man, I need to make a call ASAP!!! It's no joke." He could see that Black wasn't messing him around like the rest of the inmates did when they wanted to call home. "For real man, it's a emergency!!"

"Johnson, I came down because you have a visit. I'll see what I can do for you after you come back."

"Who is it?" Asked Black.

"Looks like the FBI," replied the deputy. "You ready now?"

Black turns around; sticking out his hands through the food slot, so the guard could slap the cuffs on. When he was secure, the officer signals to his co-worker in the control booth to open the cell. Black steps back as the cell opens, and then both of them heads up the hallway to the **attorney/client room**.

"Mr. Johnson, have a seat," says a well dressed white Detective in a suit. He had neatly combed hair and a long sharp noise. Before sitting down, Black gave the other detectives in the room a menacing stare. Clearing his throat, Detective Daniels sat down on the edge of the table, directly in front of Black.
"We're just here to touch bases with you and bring you up to date on what's going on." The detective rubs his temples.

"Lamont Bonds was killed last night," he stated bluntly, then pointed his finger. "And you could have prevented it from happening!"

Burning up inside, Black put his face in his hands and wept. Extremely distressed by the bad news, Black sat there in mute misery while the Detective went on.

"I know you're disappointed, Mr. Johnson, but crying isn't gonna help you at all. What are you gonna do now? We have no case without your friend. What else do you have for us?"

Black looks up at Daniels and says, "is he dead for real?"

The detective mutters furiously under his breath as he turns to fellow agent standing by the wall. Once Detective Daniels receives the confirmation he was looking for, he turns back to Black after agent Strickland hands him a thick, white envelope.

"You wanna know if he's dead?" The detective fumbles through the pictures until he finds it. "Here we go." Then he hands Black a 4X6 photo of his deceased friend.

Black stares at the picture in a state of shock, refusing to accept the fact that his life long buddy had departed.

"Goddamn mane, y'all ain't had to do him like that." LA was shot to smithereens. Chills radiated throughout Black's body as he viewed the gaping, blood-filled craters the police put in his man's head. His face suddenly turned the color of lava and his eyes flashed bolts of lightening.

"Y'all motherfuckers ain't had to do him like that!"

The men in the room eyed the young killer, surprised at his sudden uproar.

"What!" Black says and grills Agent Strickland. He balls the picture up and throws it.

"Better watch it now boy!" Remarks Strickland.

"Fuck you nigga! I got your boy hanging motherfucker!"

Turning red as the devil, Strickland still manages to keep a smirk on his face to hide the anger brewing inside.

"Hold it now fellas!" Shouted Daniels, holding his hand up. "Everyone needs to calm down."

Focusing his attention back on Black, "we didn't do this, so don't go pointing your finger at us. Lamont Bonds got just what he deserved. You don't go around shooting police officers. One of our cops is lying in the hospital paralyzed."

Black laughs coldly at the detective, and then glares up at him with eyes that are beyond heartless. "I wished the motherfuckers had died!" He yelled this insanely, while staring at all the men in the room. Black wanted them to know that he gave a rat's ass about a wounded cop. With LA dead, he knew that the streets were just a memory now.

For a split second, the room was so quiet that mice could be heard roaming. "I'm gonna forget you said that," Daniels counters. He looked over his shoulder at his partner. "Tell the guard to come get this son-of-a-bitch! We're wasting our time." Before he could say another word out of his mouth, Black jumps up and grabs the detective's nuts and applies pressure. The man let go of a piercing cry. With the handcuffs on, Black could only do but so much. He held on to the man's testicles, while agents tried to punish him. They beat Black so badly that when he finally did let go, neither he nor the Detective could stand.

Daniels had to leave out on a stretcher, while Black laid there with three broken ribs and spitting blood out from his mouth. He was in pain, but it wasn't physical pain. He'd lost the only true friend he'd ever had, along with his freedom. He didn't want to live without LA, and wished that the police had guns in the room so they could've shot him. Barely conscious, Black looks up at the enraged agents as he's being hauled out of the jail on a stretcher. He manages to say, "**y'all can't kill me, I'm already dead...**"

The Ghost

CHAPTER 3

17th Street Jail was on laid back status. For the first time in a long time, the jail seemed to be calm. There was little or no communication between jail inmates and even the deputies behaved with a little human decency. Many of the guys there were affected by the loss of the six individuals killed in the previous night's shootout. Throughout the jail, brothers were stunned after viewing the faces of their fallen soldiers on the news. The Mayor of the city even got on television and addressed the warfare waged between the involved. He went on to discuss the police being shot in the line of duty, but nobody got a chance to hear it. Diddy changed the channel and shouted out, "fuck the police!"

On the South side tier, the biggest disappointment was Pierre's face flashing across the screen. Many of the guys he'd bonded with while there, couldn't believe it was him. He'd gotten released only a week earlier for God sakes!

"Naw, not my nigga," Light skinned, cat eye Tyrone remarked, stunned at the bad news. "Goddamn, dude just left here!" Pierre and Tyrone bunked together the entire sixteen months they were at the city jail. Every day, they would politic about going home and making a shit load of dough. He was hurt. The two had become like the best of friends before Pierre left.

When Diddy walked over with a cup of jail house hooch in hand, Tyrone was in a trance. "Damn homey, snap out of that shit cuz. You zoned the fuck out."

"Yeah, a nigga jive fucked up," Tyrone replied.

"I feel you. Thinking about the homey, Pierre I'm guessing. Why don't you try some of this shit?" Diddy gave him a dose of the magic potion.

Tyrone put it to his mouth and sipped. "Playa, this shit better than the last batch you put down," Tyrone complemented, taking a bigger swig than the last.

"LA meant he was gone get that nigga Bernard, didn't it?" Asked Diddy.

"Yeah, homeboy was about his business. Want the rest of this?"
"Naw, go ahead and kill the rest of that," said Diddy. "I'm about to go and spark up this joint in a minute."

"Just can't believe my man got himself jammed up like that... Damn!! His mama fucked up, I know she is. She was crazy bout that Negro. She had his canteen straight the entire time he was in. Aye, what up with the nigga, Prince though? I ain't seen him all day?"

"O G messed up. You know LA was his man. I was watching Prince when they showed the homey L A's face on the news." Diddy shook his head. "O G was about to break. He went in his cell after that and ain't been back out since."

"Oh yeah?" Tyrone said surprisingly.

"If I was him, I wouldn't be mad," adds Diddy as an afterthought. "With LA out the way, they ain't got no case against the O G. The big homey ready to go raise up, watch what I tell you!" Diddy rose to his feet. "I'm going to smoke this joint, you coming?"

Immediately, Tyrone jumped up and said, "what the fuck type question is that?" They both disappeared into the section where everyone used to smoke.

Meanwhile, Prince stood in the doorway of his cell watching everyone from a distance. He pondered playing a game of dominoes with his older buddy Smitty but changed his mind. He just didn't feel like being around anyone. Part of him felt relieved to know that there was a good possibility he'd be going home, providing the Feds didn't pull another trick out of their sleeves. Then it hit him; he had just lost a good brother.

Reminiscing about L A's death was a form of torture. So many lives lost, Prince almost felt guilty to know that he could possibly be free at his next court date. Straining to hold back the tide of emotions, Prince painfully realized that just maybe, he could have pushed LA a little harder to get out of the game. He felt responsible in a sense, plus he knew for sure now, that LA never would've crossed him. But what the fuck did that matter now! **He was gone.... Damn!**

The Ghost

CHAPTER 4

Mrs. Diane was sitting in her living room, looking through old photos and baby pictures of her son. Living alone was hell at a time like this. Her sister had been over ever since yesterday, helping her cope with the terrible news and she was miserable the minute she left. Diane thought about the detective who told her this would happen. He was the last person she wanted to see. She could hear him now saying, "**I told you so.**" Instead, someone else ended up coming in his place, but by that time, she already knew her child had passed. It was painful putting on an act as if she were finding out for the first time, but necessary in order to protect Jeffery.

Never did Diane imagine she'd be on the telephone making arrangements to have her son buried, going to a funeral home and picking out a casket for the child she'd carried in her womb. Despite what the detective said, she never truly believed it could happen to her. A million times, she asked herself where she went wrong in raising him. She'd worked her hardest to keep him clothed and fed, and no matter what, he always had a place to lay his head.

The streets claimed so many lives. Some said AIDS was the number one killer in the black community. If that was true, then the streets had to be next on the list. Diane still refused to believe he did all the things the news had reported. "I raised him better than that," she kept telling herself. She couldn't help but think about the conversation she and Angie's mother had. Now she understood the pain Shannon must have felt to lash out at her the way she did.

Diane missed her son deeply. She never got a chance to talk to him and find out what he was really going through. Sick of crying, she proceeded to shut the picture album when she heard a car's engine out front. She smiled from ear to ear, watching Jeffery and that sweet girl who was with him the other night approach the house. She was excited about having company and rushed to the door, opening it before they could ring the doorbell. "Isn't this a nice surprise."

"Aye Mrs. Diane, how you doing?" Jeffery greeted her with a huge hug and kiss on the cheek.

"Hey sweetie and I didn't get your name the last time you were here darling."

"Tiffany," she replied, smiling like a little girl. Jeffrey immediately took hold of the picture album as they sat down on the sofa.

"I have some ice tea in the fridge, y'all want some?" Both answered yes simultaneously. Diane smiled easily before vanishing into the kitchen. A couple minutes later, she returned, carrying a tray with three large glasses of fresh cold tea. Diane could clearly see the love Jeffery had for her son. She plopped down on her comforter across from him, observing the two while they admired L A's pictures.

"Jeffery, you know we need pallbearers for Lamont." He nearly chokes on his drink at the statement. Tiffany eyes him suspiciously.

"What's wrong?" Diane asked as his actions clearly showed something was disturbing him.

Clearing his throat, "It's just that... I didn't think you were having a funeral."

"Now Jeffery, why wouldn't you think I'd give my son a funeral?"

"I don't mean it like that. It's not you. LA wouldn't want a funeral. He hated funerals, Mrs. Diane. He always talked about being cremated if he died."

Diane becomes uptight and starts fidgeting with her hands.
"He never told you how he felt about funerals?" Jeffery inquired. She drifted off and reflected back on earlier talks with her son. Diane would cringe inside whenever he'd start yapping about hating funerals and

being cremated. She'd simply shut him down and tell him that she didn't want to hear it. But she asked him once what his deal with funerals was.

His response was, "**funerals are fake. People you don't even know or deal with in life, come to see you when you all messed up. Their favorite line is, 'Oh, he was aight.' Naw mane, don't let nobody see me like that.**"

Diane wipes away tears as she recalls the conversation. She never took him seriously when he talked crazy like that; never thought the day would come. He was supposed to be burying her, not vice versa. Now, here he was, lying in a pine box at the same funeral home Angie was in, not even a month before. Looking away from Jeffery and Tiffany, Diane nodded her head. She hated to admit that Jeffery had corroborated her son's statement.

"Mrs. Diane, I know you don't wanna cremate your son, but he wouldn't have it any other way. You can't worry about what people gone say. Whatever you decide, I'm with you. But I gotta keep it real with you. Having a service.... Would only be a disservice to LA."

"Jeffery, what am I suppose to do? I already made arrangements to have the service in next week. I put a deposit down on the casket."

"I'll get the deposit back," replied Jeffery. "Mrs. Diane, all you want is for your son to rest in peace. We must respect his wishes. He wants to be cremated and nothing else. That's the only way he'll rest, trust me," he said reassuringly.

"You really think that's what he wanted?

"I don't think Mrs. Diane, I know."

'He's right,' Diane thought. "Oh Lord," she uttered out. "Alright Jeffery."

Looking relieved, the youngster jumped up, giving Diane another hug and kiss. Tiffany followed and then headed out the door afterwards, leaving Jeffery and Diane standing in the doorway talking. He was on his way out when out of the blue; she asked how his sisters were doing.

"*Shit,*" he mumbled under his breath, wishing like hell he'd left with Tiffany. For a few seconds, he stood there, throat too raw with pain for him to even speak. Diane witness a sadness in his eyes that made her regret asking.

"I guess uh............... I guess they doing okay. I don't' even know Mrs. Diane." His head drooped to the floor in shame. Realizing she had struck a nerve, she backed off. It was obvious from Jeffery's reaction that the subject made him uncomfortable.

Diane thought about Jeffrey's sisters long after he'd left. "**That boy in some pain,**" she noted to herself.... A person had to have experienced true pain to recognize it. Diane could relate all too well.

CHAPTER 5

Back in Gray Stone projects, a celebration was taking place, dedicated to everyone who wasn't there. Hustlers flirted with the scores of fine females who attended. The plan was to limit invitations to the hood, but as soon as the word got out about a party being held for LA and the other deceased, people swarmed from everywhere to show up and pay their respects.

Gray Stone was a grim place, so normally outsiders would exercise extreme caution when visiting, especially after dark. Tonight was different. It wasn't a pity party, but a celebration with good music, liquor and girls; it most certainly was going to be a blast. Most of the ballers stopped by the liquor store to buy their own alcohol, including an extra bottle to pour out for the fallen soldiers.

The chicks gathered around the big crap game, scoping out the deep pockets. It just wasn't the same without LA. He brought gambling to life. People came just to hear him bully his opponents. Marijuana appeared legalized the way smokers sparked freely. Jeffrey loved every minute of it. The entire party was comatose from the exotic weed he had. Over forty pounds of the best smoke in the city, Jeffrey had some of the biggest names in the streets coming to him to get accommodated. Because of the exceptional quality of it, no one disputed or ever complained. They simply wanted quality shit. Jeffrey had made over six grand already, and the night was still young. When LA first gave him the two monster bags of weed, he didn't know what the hell he'd do with it.

Feeling a buzz, Jeffrey stood directly in front of the same vacant apartment where he had been previously robbed. He held the Glock on his waist side, wide open, and leaning on the wall as he kicked it with his high school buddy, Eco. Jeffrey gazed up and down the street at all the nice whips lined up, leaving no parking spaces.

19

"Damn cuz, this motherfucker jumping," Eco said excitedly, hawking a champagne colored Lexus filled with chicks, as it pulled over in the middle of the street to flirt at a pack of hungry hustler's shooting dice on the steps. Jeffrey couldn't help but notice a pretty young chick checking him out from afar. 5' 6" with light brown eyes, Keisha was the prettiest girl in the whole school. He scanned the scene, searching for Tiffany. He spotted her across the street talking to Angie's sister, Shonda.

Keisha was aware that Jeffrey was with Tiffany and laughed to herself, knowing she was the only obstacle standing in the way of him coming over. She continued to drive him crazy, blowing kisses and running her tongue over her lips as if she were imagining something delicious in her mouth.

'Something was different,' Keisha thought. It was Jeffrey's demeanor. He was nothing like this at school.

"Bitch fucking up my program," uttered Keisha as she rolled her eyes at Tiffany. The girls beside her yapping, she paid no attention to. Until now, she had never even considered Jeffrey. At school, there was none of this thuggish, loud and obnoxious behavior. But she admired the more thug appeal better. Staring at the cash in his hand, she thought, "Damn, that nigga done came up!"

"You see that shit Eco? She doing it again," Jeffrey said amped up about honey from school giving him mad play.

"Yeah, I saw her that time, "Eco replied.

"Damn, she trying to fuck tonight, ain't she? Look like the whole crew trained to go. Damn nigga, what you gone do?"

"Not a damn thing with Tiffany standing right there watching me. She thinks she slick too." The two laughed at Jeffrey's statement.

"Aight, bet!"

"**Umm, umm, ummph**... Keisha pretty ass can get it. I gotta fuck that

20

bitch tonight. Look at her. She wide open with that shit!" Jeffrey chuckled. "Ain't give a nigga no play in school. Now look at her. She must peeped my bankroll." Jeffrey sat there imagining himself banging her back out and simply having his way with her.

"Damn cuz, fuck all this staring shit! You want me to go holla at shorty or what?" Eco asked, more than eager to set something up for later.

Jeffrey contemplated the idea for a moment. "Yeah, see what's up with her. If she trying to get at a nigga, tell her to meet me on the back street in 30 minutes." He laughed watching Eco take off without a word. Jeffrey headed in the opposite direction toward the crap game. He approached the crowd, giving everyone he knew dap, and others head nods. As he stand over the shooters, his mind drifts off into space. "Damn, my niggas suppose to be out here."

Was Jeffrey high or did he hear his man LA talking shit? "**Hit dice!**" Shouted the shooter as he rolled the dice.

"Damn, I must be tripping. Miss that nigga." Jeffrey looked around through the crowd of faces and thought he saw Black posted up quietly, observing the whole scene like some type of guard. He blinked his eyes. Ducky, the cat he'd mistaken for Black, was now staring back at him, wondering what the hell was on Jeffrey's mind.

"Let me get the fuck from over here." Jeffrey walks off.

Eco comes rushing up excited. "It's on nigga!! They are waiting on us now. Oh, I bagged the red bone beside her. Damn, I done forgot her name already. Keisha say don't be bull shitting either. Ebony, that's her name!"

"I gotta holla at Tiff right quick. Go get the stash and meet me at my spot in ten minutes."

Jeffrey heads toward Tiffany and her entourage of project chicks, vicious broads who rolled up at parties, strapping anything from razors to automatics pistols. He hated when Tiffany hung around with her girls.

The Ghost

"Tiffany! Tiffany!" He hollered her name out from a couple of yards away, not trying to go near her **she-thugs**. Jeffrey watched as she made her way over to him, admiring her sexy walk.

'Damn she looking fine,' he thought. But tonight, Keisha was holding the spotlight down. "Aye, what you over there doing?"

Tiffany blushes. "Just over there talking to their crazy asses."

Walking up the street arm-in-arm like a young couple, Jeffrey turned to his girl and pulled out money from all four of his pockets.

"Here, put this in your pocketbook. I got some shit I need to do. Take it in the house and count it. I'll call you when I get back, aight?"

"OK, give me a kiss, "Tiffany said, puckering her lips, waiting for his to connect. Jeffrey hugs his girl and gives her a quick peck on the lips.

"Aight now, take your ass home and count that dough," he jokes and slaps her on her backside.

Tiffany returns a perfect smile. "Don't forget to call me," she hollers over her shoulder, and makes her way up the sidewalk to her apartment. Jeffrey glance over at Keisha and signals for her to go to the spot. She quickly whispers something to her girlfriend beside her. Minutes later, they get inside their vehicle and drive off.

Blocks from the projects, Keisha and two girls sat in a cherry red Acura Legend, waiting to get their freak on. Her face lowers upon glancing in the rear view at Jeffrey exiting the passenger door, coming up to her.

"What's good shorty? You gone chill out with a nigga or what?"

"I'm here, ain't it? I see your girl let you come out to play." Her friends laugh out loud.

Jeffrey gives her a phony smile, then reaches in his pocket and hands her money to purchase a room. "Go head and get a room, I gotta stop somewhere first, call me and let me know where you at, aight?"

"Aight," she responds in a sexy, feminine tone. "Don't keep me waiting too long."

Jeffrey stares lustfully down at her thick thighs.

"Bring some weed," Keisha adds.

"Oh you ain't heard... I'm that nigga?" He hollers and heads back to Eco's ride. "I got that," he hollers back at her as he opens the passenger door and hops in.

After stashing the weed he didn't get a chance to sale, Jeffrey and Eco headed up to the La Quinta Hotel. Sunk low in the passenger seat, Jeffrey sipped the fifth of Hennessey while looking out the window at the passing cars in a daze. They make a right turn off Warwick Road onto a dark residential street. As Eco drives the speed limit, Jeffrey's eyes locks in on a guy sporting a yellow and purple Lakers fitted cap with oil stained Timberland boots on his feet. Smiling to himself, Jeffrey turns to Eco, his eyes wide with excitement.

"My nigga, pull over right quick. Right here. Hurry up!!"

"What's up?" Eco ask and pulls over. He's totally confused and shocked at Jeffrey's mysterious behavior. Jeffrey pushes open the door and jumps out while the car is still rolling.

"What the fuck mane? What you doing?"

"Nothing, just wait right there. I be back in a minute."

With that said, off Jeffrey goes moving swiftly in the opposite direction, leaving Eco dumbfounded. The streets was dark and deserted with the exception of a glimmer coming from the dim street lights. Quietly, he crosses the street steps ahead of the stranger. When they are five feet apart, Jeffrey calls out, "slim, you got a light?"

Stopping in his tracks, the man searches his pockets for matches as Jeffrey comes to stand directly in front of him.

"Here you go stick mane." Finding the matches, the man extends out his hand for Jeffrey to take them.

"You smoke these cuz?" Asked Jeffrey.

The guy looks up to answer Jeffrey and immediately places the face. At the mere sight of the menacing glare, he ends up dropping the matches, along with his jaw at the same time, staring frantically down the barrel of Jeffrey's nickel plated 9 mm.

"Come on now lil shorty, don't take it personal. You know a nigga was sick." The man pleads. Without another second to spare, Jeffrey points the pistol to his chest and fires four slugs, sending him crashing to the pavement. He then pulls out a twenty dollar bill and tosses it on what is left of the guy's bullet riddled body and spats on him.

"**Bitch ass nigga**! Bet you won't rob nobody else!" Jeffrey coldly states before dashing up the street to his buddy's waiting ride.

Eco was stunned. He'd witnessed the entire event from his rear view mirror, wondering what the hell had snapped inside his childhood friend. The Jeffrey he knew didn't even like guns, so to see him snuff someone out so coldly, totally blew him. Breathing heavily, Jeffrey snatches open the passenger door and jumps in the car, facing Eco hyped.

"You ready to go see those hoes? Let's go nigga, what you waiting on?"

Speechless, Eco throws the car in gear, put his foot on the gas pedal and punches it!"

CHAPTER 6

His face was balled up. "Why do you gotta look like that?" Wanda asked in a concerned tone as she gazed through the dull, fingerprinted covered Plexiglas.

"I'm good," replied Prince. "Just got some shit on my mind, that's all." She hated when she didn't have his undivided attention.
"You thinking about LA, ain't you?"

Knowing she would keep digging, Prince breathed easily before answering. "Yeah, I'm jive fucked up baby."

"Damn," she was sympathetic. "I know how you felt about him. Prince, I don't know what to say. If you want, I'll go check on his mama for you. What do you think about her cremating that boy?"

Prince didn't seem the least bit surprised. He just smiled at Wanda. "That's what the boy wanted," he replied with confidence.

Wanda smacked her lips at Prince's response as if he didn't know what the hell he was saying. "What do you mean, that's what he wanted?"

Prince tried to be patient with Wanda and her million and one questions. "We use to kick it about shit like that. He told me a rack of times that if he ever died, he wanted to be cremated. He didn't think his mama would do it though."

"Prince, I know you upset," Wanda said as both of them stare into one another's eyes. Her tone becomes slower and more feminine. "You look so good when you smile."

"Is that right?" Prince asked and sat up straight.

"I can't wait until you get home boy... I swear. So many things I wanna do to you."

"Girl, don't start that. Got my shit over here throbbing already."

"Aight then, let me leave you alone." She flushes with delight. "I got a surprise for you."

"What's that? Hope it's something wet and taste like candy," Prince reply in a whisper, trying not to let his jail buddies next to him hear his wish.

"Close your eyes," Wanda commands.

"You about to get butt naked boo?"

"You won't find out until you close your eyes, now will you?" She remarks in a husky and seductive tone.

Like a good little boy, Prince did as he was told. Seconds later, a tap on the window got his attention. He opened his eyes, squinted and then snatched the receiver, placing it against his ear in a burst of excitement.

"**Jeffrey, my nigga!** What a nice surprise." He looks over Jeffrey's shoulder at Wanda and blows her a kiss.

"It's good to see you. What's good?" Prince recognizes the blood shot eyes immediately. Any other time, he would've checked the youngster, but at the moment, it didn't even matter.

"Ain't shit, just left the mall, and brought my sisters a couple things."

"Oh yeah, how they doing?"

Jeffrey's facial expression changes. "Prince mane, so much shit been happening. I ain't even had a chance to check on them." He stares the O G in the eyes. "A nigga been going through it out here mane."

Prince listened to the young buck kick it about the shootout with Bernard and how LA saved his life by letting him wear the vest.

"Jeffrey, you gotta slow down out there man. Just hold fast until I touchdown."

"I feel you mane, but I'm gone be homeless in another two weeks," Jeffrey replied. "They saying I need a guardian living with me."

"Don't even sweat that playa. I got a spot for you. Go ahead and put your shit in storage. You got money?"

"Yeah, I'm straight."

"Aye... Chill! You wilding the fuck out! I should be home on my next court date and we gone get your sisters back. It may take a little time, but they gone be aight." Prince grins and shakes his head. "I feel you... But you gotta fall back though."

"Thanks Prince, mane. I'm out here waiting on you." Wanda walks in giving the indication that Jeffrey's time was up.

"Aye mane, I'll holla back," Jeffrey says and stands. "Come over here girl," he hollers out to Tiffany. Prince leans over to see who he's calling. His eyes light up at the sight of the pretty young teenager.

'Damn... They sure don't make them like they use to,' thought Prince

.

Tiffany takes the phone from Jeffrey to say a few words then she gives the phone back to Wanda. The young couple waves goodbye before exiting through the door, leaving Wanda alone with Prince to finish fanta-sizing about his release.

The Ghost

CHAPTER 7

After leaving the city jail, Jeffrey decides to go and check on his friend Black as well. It seemed like forever since he had last seen him, so he headed straight over to Henrico jail only to discover that Black's visiting day had already passed. Slightly disappointed, Jeffrey steps aside, retrieving from his pocket a bankroll. He lifts a couple of franks off the roll to leave to his friend.

"What is his name?" Asked the female deputy.

"Barry Johnson." Jeffrey hesitated, trying to remember his middle name to no avail.

She concentrated on the screen in front of her, combing through the vast list of names. Then Jeffrey recalled Black's middle initials started with the letter N, which helped the deputy locate his friend immediately. She gazed into the screen for a few moments and looks up at Jeffrey. "I'm sorry sir, but Johnson is no longer here."

Dumbfounded, Jeffrey replies, "what you mean not here?"

The young attractive deputy smiles. "I'm not permitted to release any information on inmates."

Clearly disappointed and confused, Jeffrey was surprised. "He was just here!" The lady was sympathetic to Jeffrey's situation, realizing that he was possibly a concerned family member. All she would reveal to Jeffrey was that Black had gotten in some trouble and had to be shipped to another facility.

The ride to South side was quiet. Frustrated, Jeffrey snapped at Tiffany for asking a million and one questions. Everything just seemed to be going wrong in his life and there wasn't any relief in sight. He felt lost and alone with the death of his mother. And then there was Angie and LA and where the fuck was Black? The only comfort in his life at this point was the fact that Prince could possibly be home soon. It was all he had to look forward to.

Jeffrey focused on the piece of paper in his hand while Tiffany listened as he directed her to their next destination.

"Make that right coming up on Iron Bridge," he instructed her while staring out the window. Riding slowly down the street, Tiffany monitored her side while Jeffrey watched his.

"Slow down, slow down! I think this the place right here." Again, he looked down at the address, then back at the huge two-story brick structure. *It was the facility where his sisters were being held.*

"Yeah, this gotta be the place." After taking a deep breath, Jeffrey opens the door and steps out of the car. With Tiffany by his side, they stroll up the walkway. She smiles at the three adorable kids who flutters by them. One little girl appears to be between six and seven years old. Her hair hung to her back and when she smiled, her tonsils showed through three missing teeth.

Tiffany approached the front entrance and held the door open for Jeffrey only to find him staring, mesmerized in the opposite direction. She called out to him.

"Come on boy, what are you doing?" When he didn't answer, she walked back over to stand next to him.

"Look, look!" Jeffrey exclaimed and pointed over toward an enormous playground. Children were playing chase, taking turns on the sliding board; laughing and simply being kids. In the sand by the monkey bars, two teenagers were pushing each other, commencing to fight. Ten yards from the monkey bars, his eyes zeroed in on one girl pushing another in the middle swing. There were no other kids around them.

"Look at them." Jeffrey's mouth curls into a pleasant smile and his eyes glitters with admiration as his heart flush and tears comes to surface. **The girls were his long sisters.** "Ericaaaa!! Brittneyyy!!!"

Immediately, Erica's head turns with breakneck speed, using her hand as a visor to the beaming sun. She held the swing in an effort to prevent it from crashing into her as she focused on the familiar voice. The siblings hadn't seen one another in months, which seemed like years, so upon them reuniting, there was a tremendous amount of emotion. Britney blurts out, "**that's our brother!**" And then she took off toward him, Erica on her heels, choking back tears.

Children being housed in the facility stood around watching the emotional reunion as Jeffrey holstered his adorable baby sister from the ground and showered her with a bunch of kisses. Erica cried like a baby. All the weeks of trying to be strong, holding back tears for Brittney, had taken its toll on Erica and so finally, she allowed herself to cry. She'd been so worried about her brother that it had begun to drive her nuts! L A's death only added to her grief. She didn't associate with any of the girls who lived with her and never let Brittney out of her sight.

"Jeffrey, are you gonna stay with us?" Asked Brittney.

He responded with a hug. How could he find the words to say that he'd have to leave without them? The threesome walked over to the picnic table and sat down.

"Boy, I've been worrying myself to death." Erica wiped her eyes. "Are your fingers broke or something? You know we need to hear from you." Brittney sat in between, looking at Erica when she spoke, then back at Jeffrey waiting on his response.

Jeffrey dropped his head in shame. He fought back tears that seemed to choke the life out of him. She was right and there was nothing he could say. "Erica, I know I should be hollering at y'all more." Hesitating, he chose his words carefully so as not to disturb his sisters. He saw no need in burdening her with what he had going on in the streets, so all he could muster out was, "shorty, if only you knew what I been going through out here." Jeffrey expressed, pondering over the limp body he'd left slumped not even 24 hours ago.

"What happen to LA?" Erica was crazy about LA. She had a crush on him ever since she was a little girl.

"The police shot him," Jeffrey states plainly. It was a long story, and he definitely didn't feel up to traveling back down that painful road right now. Changing the subject, he went into their living conditions.

"So how these people treating you?"

"I wanna go home Jeffrey, "Brittney cried out, clinging to her brother's neck. Erica watched her sister throw a fit.

"Now you see what I go through every day," Erica states shaking her head.

"Shhhhh... We gone be aight." Jeffrey whispers repeatedly in her ear.

"Prince says he gone help me get y'all back."

"For real?" Erica jumps up excitedly.

Brittney stops crying and focus her undivided attention on her brother. "That mean we coming home?"

"Yeah baby girl, but it's going to take some time," Jeffrey tried to explain.

Erica took a seat back on the table. "Jeffrey, how long you think it'll take?"

"He'll be home in a month." A deep breath, he faced his sister. "Erica, don't think for one minute that I forgot about y'all. Every move I make has to do with y'all. I'm struggling out here sis, but shit gone get better soon. Just give me a little time okay?"

Erica's eyes sparkled with happiness as she held out her hand for his. He looked down at Brittney.

"You gone give your big brother some time too?"

Brittney shrieked with excitement. "How longgggg?"

Jeffrey grins. "Not long," he reply and kiss her puffy cheeks. He glances over his shoulder and sees Tiffany talking to a middle aged meaty, black woman.

"Who is that lady over there?"

"Oh, that's my case worker. She real cool," replied Erica. "Come on, she wants to meet you."

Jeffrey hesitated a moment, reached down into his pocket for money and slid her a roll of twenty dollar bills. Pop eyed at the sight of the cash, she quickly stashed it in her bra, and then the three of them headed over toward Tiffany and the caseworker.

"Oh, I bought y'all something from the mall."

"You bought me something Jeffrey?" Brittney asks happily.

"I hope it ain't clothes," Erica remarks laughing.

"Tiffany knows your size right?"

"Oh yeah, thank God. We use to wear the same size."

"Good, because she picked them out."

"Hi Mrs. Anderson, this is my brother," Erica says proudly.

"Hey girl," Tiffany happily belts and hugs Erica.

"So, this is Jeffrey." Mrs. Anderson says and observes the young man. "I've heard so much about you."

"How you doing Mrs. Anderson. I hope you heard something good."

Everyone laughs. All of a sudden, her tone becomes serious. "Your sister's really loves you." Jeffrey turns to them both.

"And I love them." Brittney clings to his hand.

"Jeffrey, I'll get the bags out the trunk for them." Tiffany offered and then she, Erica and Brittney proceeds off, leaving the caseworker and Jeffrey to talk in private. The minute they were alone, Mrs. Anderson turned to Jeffrey. "What are you doing now that you aren't in school?"

The youngster was speechless. He thought, **'she knows damn well what I'm out here doing!'** He started to speak when she interrupted.

"Don't even answer that question," she replied with a smirk. Jeffrey let out an appreciative sigh. "Just know that you have two beautiful sisters. Everything you do affects them so be careful."

Jeffrey agreed. "You right Mrs. Anderson. It's hard, but I'm striving to do the right thing."

"Well, that's all you can do is try your best, right? How you holding up? I've been working with your sisters, and Erica kind of confides in me. I have to ask. I'm just curious to know how you're coping with the loss of your mother, sisters and now your friends. It has to be hard."

"Honestly, I don't know how I'm coping."

It was a question that he'd never been asked before and he was instantly moved to tears. They came out of nowhere. *'I honestly don't know how I manage to last this long. There ain't a morning that I don't wake up, look over at my Glock on the dresser and contemplate ending my miserable existence. Everyone is gone. One day everyone is here and its love and then suddenly, you look up and it's just you. This is my life... I'm not coping... I'm running...* Jeffrey thinking out loud...*Would she even understand?*

"It's a struggle Mrs. Anderson. Is it aight if I come back to visit my sisters?"

"Sure, but only on the weekends. I made an exception today because I knew they needed to see you."

"Thank you."

"You're welcome. I'll let you go. We'll talk another time. You be careful now." Mrs. Anderson turned and walked back to the building.

Brittney ran up and hugged her brother. "Thank you Jeffrey, I love the clothes you bought."

"You welcome sweetie."

Erica's hands were full. He took the bags and walked the girls up to the front door, pausing to give his sisters another heartfelt hug.

"I'll be back next week, aight." The child nods her head as he kneels to hug and kiss her.

"I'm coming back to get you, OK? I promise you baby girl," Jeffrey assured as he struggled to hold back tears. "**I-gotta-go-okay**... See y'all later."

"We love you Jeffrey," Erica yells as he hurriedly tries to run off before they could see his tears. Tiffany immediately tries to console Jeffrey as he sat inside the car and began to sob intensely. "**Just drive. Please... Just get me out of here!**"

The Ghost

CHAPTER 8

Physicians at Chippenham Hospital recommended Detective Daniels be hospitalized until the pain subsided in his testicles. When he first arrived, they couldn't find any difficulties, although he indicated he was feeling extreme discomfort. They told his wife it would be a good idea to keep him overnight to monitor his condition. The next morning he awakened and started to get up to use the restroom. When Daniels moved his leg, a sharp pain shot through his entire body, causing him to shriek loud enough that his wife jumped from the chair she was sleeping on.

"Get the nurse!" He managed to utter painfully as he lay paralyzed. He lifted the sheet up and almost had a heart attack. Daniel's testicles had swollen up to the size of two tennis balls. His wife rushed back in, followed by the doctor. She moved so fast she had forgotten that all she had to do was mash the button on the side of the bed.

"What's the problem?" The young, pencil nose doctor asked calmly as he stood over the detective. He could see that something was obviously wrong from the discomforting expression on Daniel's face.

"Let me take a quick look," he says lifting the sheet back. Curious, his wife stands directly behind him, trying to catch a glimpse.

"Good Lord," the doctor and the detective's wife exclaimed simultaneously as they gawked down at the world's largest nut sacks! Embarrassed, Daniels snatches the sheet back over himself. His wife snickers and falls back on the couch. Pencil nose smirks as if he'd saw something pleasant. Daniels is seconds away from flickering off.

"Aren't you glad we kept you overnight? This was the very reason I didn't want to release you."

"Is it serious, Doc? Why are they so huge?" Asked the detective. He glared evilly at his wife upon catching her smiling. The doctor also found the question amusing and tried his hardest to muzzle his laughter, but the wife wasn't making it any easier.

Clearing his throat, he apologized to the detective and explained that he had nothing to worry about.

"The pain and swelling you're experiencing is normal. Testicles are one of the most sensitive organs in the body. The test results show no indication of any internal damage. However, swelling is to be expected. Not to worry though, the anti-inflammatory should knock the swelling right out. As for the pain, I'll give you some Percocet's. You'll feel as good as new in a minute. The nurse will be right back with your dosage."

After the doctor left, Daniels rolled over to his wife and asked what was so funny. She gave him a juicy kiss.

"You think it's funny, don't you? Here it is, my nuts done swelled up the size of plums, and you and pencil nose finds it funny!"

"I'm sorry sweetheart," she says between laughs. "I'm just happy it isn't serious."

"Yeah, I bet." A knock at the door got their attention.

Detective Rasheed peeked in the room. "If y'all busy, I can come back."

"Ah, cut it out," replied Daniels.

Rasheed closed the door behind him with a smile on his face.

"How's your nuggets, sir? I mean... Well you know."

"Go to hell detective!" He glanced over at his wife, who was turning red from laughter.

"Goddamn circus in here. I'm getting tired of all the jokes! What brings you here? I'm sure you didn't come all the way down to make nut jokes."

"Sorry detective, uh...." Rasheed's face becomes serious. "Percy Miller's attorney has been calling the D A's office asking for a dismissal. He's threatening to file a motion with the courts to have his client released immediately, instead of waiting for the scheduled date."

Before Daniel's could respond, the nurse enters the room. "Here you go sir." She hands him two pain pills and waits while he takes them, then she turns and flutters out of the room.

Focusing his attention back on Rasheed, he continues. "I'm not surprised... Unless someone else comes forth saying they purchased drugs from Miller, or knew something about those homicides, he's a free man. Lucky son of a bitch beat us again! Wait a minute! What's that kid's name?"

"Jeffrey Owen's," Rasheed answered. "Good kid, been through hell. I hear he's pretty tight with Prince. Why you ask?"

"Remember, they were at the hospital when his mother was shot? What you think, detective?" Rasheed studies the question. "Honestly sir, I really think nothing of it. School kid, probably never even sold drugs a day in his life."

"**If you ask me, all those sons of bitches sale drugs,**" Daniels states harshly, clearly still upset about the altercation with Black. "Remember detective... All that was before his mother died. What's he doing now?"

Rasheed grins devilishly. "That's a good question."

The Ghost

CHAPTER 9

Sunk in a state of darkness, Kush smoke filled the room as Jeffrey recalled his mother's agony for the condition the community was in as a result of that **white poison**. He felt ashamed and hopeless doing it. It's the reason he stayed lifted off of weed in the first place. The thoughts were just too powerful to endure on a sober mind. He wondered if she was looking over him. God, she had to be rolling over in her grave. He did, however get comfort whenever his sisters came to mind. What could he have been thinking to wait so long to visit them? Brittney looked so pretty. And he was pleased to see how well Erica was holding up and clinging to their little sister.

Dianne honored L A's wishes. Instead of a traditional service, she decided to have a little get together at her house and everyone who loved her son was invited. Jeffrey wondered how Black was making it. He sure did miss his crazy ass. How did things become so screwed up? Everyone he knew was messed up in the game, struggling through some type of tribulation. And why the hell was Black shipped?? Jeffrey had yet to get the answer to that question.

"Oh shit! He jumps up from his bed and grabs a notebook from the dresser, almost forgetting about Blacks letter. He sat in a daze with the letter in his hand.

"This nigga dun lost his mind." He ripped the letter up and dropped it into the wastebasket in his room. Jeffrey's weed habit had increased noticeably, to the point that he was high all the time. The weed made him feel good and free from the madness that filled his life. He peered out the window and saw that the block was deserted. He thought that was odd. The Avenue was just jumping with life before he left. Jeffrey was about to slip on some fresh Butter Timberland boots when the telephone started to ring.

In a rush, Jeffrey ignored the call and proceeded to put on his boots. By the time he got them on, the ringing commenced. He walked over to the phone and looked at the caller id. "What the hell she wants..." The call was from his neighbor, Tamara who lived two doors down. Jeffrey had just sold her boyfriend, Marlo a quarter pound of smoke earlier.

"She don't won't shit." He mumbled before grabbing his Glock from the dresser.

On his way down stairs, he could hear someone trying to reach him on his cell as it chimed from his inside coat pocket. He put the phone to his ear and mumbled a couple of words at the same time he opened the front door. He froze at the sight of flashing white and blue lights and began to slowly inch back into the apartment.

"Where they at Tamara?" He utters nervously into the phone. Slamming the door shut, he hit the light switch and peers out the window blinds at two police officers shining flashlights in the bushes! From experience, the police knew dealers hid their drugs in bushes around the projects. It was routine. They'd ride through in one of their squad cars, scope out the scenery, then leave. Minutes later, there would be what Jeffrey and his crew called the **JUMP OUT SQUAD**... Three to four unmarked cars, bum rushing the spot, running down hustlers. The cops rolled deep and were more crooked than the letter C.

Jeffrey was relieved he missed the surprise entry. Outside his door, officers on the sidewalk were detaining four of his buddies. Tamara said one of the guys the police had, was her boyfriend. She was standing right outside her door, informing Jeffrey of everything they were doing. She was the one who'd been calling his house phone. When he didn't answer, she tried his cell. He picked up just in time. Five seconds later, he would've walked straight into an ambush, **gun, weed and al**l. Jeffrey took his coat off, walks back upstairs, kicks off his shoes and lay across the bed.

"**Must ain't meant to be out there tonight**," he admitted, sipping casually off a small Hennessey bottle. He glanced over at the dresser as his cell began to chirp once more. Quickly, he jumped up and mashed the button, putting it to his ear. A look of gratification covered his face as he spoke into the receiver.

"Bye."

"I ain't think you'd holla back at ol' boy," Jeffrey said, crashing on the bed and firing up some weed. "So, what's up for tonight?"

"What you want to be up?" Keisha replied.

"You enjoyed yourself the other night?"
"If I knew you were built like that, I would've been got at you."

"Oh yeah?" Jeffrey sighs as his ego skyrockets. "You try to carry a nigga in school though."

"Go ahead boy, it won't like that!"

"For real, I use to try and holla at you, but every time you'd spin me."

"I'm sorry boo. I'll make it up to you," Keisha said sounding sexy as ever.

He laughed, "I think that's a good idea because I'm feeling some type of way about that. So how you plan on making that up?"

"Can't tell you. But you'll see."

"When?"

"Now! If Tiffany ain't got handcuffs on you."

"There you go. You coming to scoop me right? Police out here, I ain't driving."

"I'll be there in 10 minutes," she giggles. "I won't have on any panties either!"

"Mmmm, good...................... You ain't need them anyway," replied

Jeffrey. "Aight, holla back."

CHAPTER 10

Ten minutes later, Keisha was sitting out in front of Jeffrey's apartment, honking her horn. Jeffrey peeks through the screen before stepping out into the dark night. In the projects, all sorts of dangers could await on that other side. Realizing that the coast was clear, Jeffrey locks the door and dashes to the jeep and jumps in. As Keisha pulls away, he glances over at her. She was prettier than before. Immediately, her sweet smell filled his nostrils.

"So, where we going?" She asked him as she came to a stop sign at the entrance of the apartments.

"Hit the highway, they got some aight rooms in Chesterfield."

Approaching Interstate 95, Jeffrey noticed the long coat she was wearing as his eyes locked in on the wide split that revealed a generous portion of her meaty thigh.

Keisha drove in silence, secretly watching him watch her through her peripheral. She could tell he wanted to play, so she slightly opened her legs, exposing even more of her milky thighs. She snickered inside at how fast his head spun.

Sliding closer, Jeffrey leaned back, placing his hand in between her soft legs while at the same time, caressing the back of her neck with the other. He kissed her gently on her neck, her face and back to her neck, making her blush and tremble. His hands searched further up her leg as he continued to work his tongue.

"Boy, you gone make me crash," she whined but never stopped him. The closer his fingers got to her wetness, the wider her legs spread.

"Damn girl, you don't got on no-"

"Told you I won't wearing any."

Jeffrey's hands were slick with her moisture and his rock hard penis was about to explode from excitement!!! He hadn't taken her seriously about her underwear comment until now.

"I gotta have it," he whispered and bit her ear! He was a fucking animal!! He discretely glided his hand pass his nose, taking in her aroma.

Keisha was super wet. She got exactly what she asked for and now she was almost begging for him to stop. He continued to stroke her clit and she desperately wanted him to stop before she wrecked her car, but it felt sooo good! Saliva leaked out of the corner of her lips as her mouth watered.

"I gotta stop! I can't drive," she moaned out.

"Pull over if you can't drive."

"Where?" Keisha couldn't wait any longer!! Her breathing had increased and it appeared as though she drove a stick shift the way she clutched Jeffrey's shaft. In the past, she wouldn't have dreamed of making out in a car but at the present, she didn't care. Keisha wanted to feel him inside of her right now! The Rest Stop was coming up on the right. She cut on the signal light and merged to the next lane.

Driving slowly through the Rest Stop parking lot, Jeffrey found a secluded area. "Right there." Jeffrey pointed beside a huge tractor trailer and a sky blue Blazer. She pulled between the two and cut off the headlights. Both of them looked around. The place was empty with the exception of a few people lingering about. With the big tractor there, it was hard for anyone to see them. Keisha was already coming out of her coat.

"Damn girl, you ain't got on nothing!" Keisha was totally nude.

"What you waiting on?" She asked reclining the seat back to make more room. She was scared and excited at the same time.

Jeffrey's jeans were down his ankles. They kissed and exchanged tongues, and then he squeezed her breasts, and ran his lips over her firm nipples. Her scent was enticing.

"I gotta taste this pussy," he mumbled out as he licked down her juicy thighs. Realizing what he was about to do, Keisha's body tensed and she moaned out his name. She grasped his hair. Jeffrey massaged her pussy with his lips, while his tongue worked like a snake against her clitoris. Her body shivers as she undergoes spasm after spasm from Jeffrey's tongue work.

It felt so good that Keisha pushed him back, lifted his shirt up and started kissing his chest. She licked and sucked his dick hungrily. Jeffrey jerked back to avoid getting a passion mark.

"Aight girl, go head with that shit!"

Keisha smiles, then grabs his dick and stuffs her mouth as though she's competing in an all you can eat contest. A few minutes later, she laid a light kiss on his head and got on top of it. The windows are fogging up, both of them sweating profusely. Jeffrey squeezes her ass cheeks while he alternates sucking both breasts. Her nails dig into his chest as she rides him slowly then fast. The rental truck is spacey. Keisha moves faster and starts to pant like a puppy as she feels her orgasm approaching.

Jeffrey can sense she is about to cum because her walls pulls him inside like a vacuum. After Keisha get hers, he turns her over and starts banging her from behind. He thought he heard sounds and slowed his pace. No one materializes, so he kept going.

"Fuck it," he says and pumps faster, determined to let no one stop him from getting his.

"Boy, somebody coming!!!! Hurry!!!" Keisha says as she tries to raise up but never stops throwing it back.
"Yeah.................... MEEEEEEEEEEEEE!!!!!!!" His knees

weakens as he erupts, filling her entire body with pleasure. Jeffrey breathes heavily, and then collapse on top of Keisha.

"We gotta get out of here," she said pushing him off of her. Both rose up from their position. Jeffrey pulled his pants up, while Keisha adjusted the seat to an upright position. She slipped her coat back on and got behind the wheel.

"Oh-my-God!!!" She yelled suddenly as she gawked out the window at the hillbilly driving the tractor trailer beside them. The guy was leaned up against his truck, eating chips he got from the vending machine. Jeffrey laughed uncontrollably.

"Ain't nothing funny," she whispers in disgust. She turned the key and cranked the engine, embarrassed and nervous. "What he looking at, ill?" Keisha blurted out in disgust.

"Probably still picturing your big ass in the air!" Jeffrey replied tickled to death.

"Go to hell," she tells him as she backs up out of the parking space and heads towards the interstate.

CHAPTER 11

Diane had one of the nicest homes in all of Laburnum Springs. She'd been living there over 10 years. It was a two-story colonial, with an enormous backyard. Three picnic tables surrounded a fishpond in the center of the yard with a work shed in the corner. LA would often pay it an occasional smoke visit or use it to count money when nowhere else was available. He had a tall, white picket fence built around the perimeter. It was a really peaceful place and all hers.

Diane had outdone herself today with three big grills, cooking everything from salmon to zucchini. It was a beautiful day and the house was filled with people. Close friends and relatives were lingering around. Kids ran loose; having themselves a blast while grown folks sipped alcoholic beverages. Music played and folks partied like it was the 80s. Diane was pleased to see her family there supporting her, including her distant crack head brother Lorenzo.

Not everyone agreed with her decision to cremate her son, and other family members almost had a fit when Diane announced that she wouldn't have a service. She already knew it wouldn't sit well with her family, but her mind was made up. When her sister Pauline had tried to talk her out of it, Diane told her off.

"This ain't about you," she said with much authority. "Nor is it about me. This is about Lamont. He wanted it like this, do you understand? If y'all can't accept that, then tough!!"

Lorenzo was the only family member to stand by her decision. The family got a huge kick out of Lorenzo staggering across the yard from the cooler, with two cans of Budweiser's in his hand. He guzzled one beer, then poured the other out into the grass. "Nephew, this is for you," Lorenzo said drunkenly as the liquor poured. The man was drunk as a skunk, but dead serious. He loved Lamont. Out of all the members in his family, LA never once looked down on him or treated him differently because of his drug addiction. LA didn't see a junkie when he looked at his uncle. To him, Lorenzo was the same person who used to drive up in the cleanest Caddy and pass out cash like it was nothing to all the project kids back in the day.

LA never forgot that, and still respected his uncle the same. He was told very early in life to always respect his elders. As a kid, uncle Lorenzo once said. "***Never look down on anybody, because the person you look down on, will be the same one you be looking up at when you're going down.***" Lorenzo dropped a ton of jewels on his nephew. He was on his way back to the cooler to get more beer when he spotted Jeffrey and about 15 of his friends crashing the party.

"**Aye there boy!**" Lorenzo hollered out trying to get Jeffrey's attention. Diane glanced up from the grill to see what all the commotion was about and was delighted to see Jeffrey's face. "Watch the hamburgers Pauline," she told her sister and walked off to greet him. When she approached Jeffrey, he was trying to break out of the bear hug Lorenzo had on him. While she stood aside, a friend of Jeffrey's, stepped in front of her and introduced himself as Ronnie. The big youngster hugged her and landed a kiss on her cheek. Then one by one, the rest of the guys followed up. They were all friends of her late son. After the last hug, Diane was smiling from ear to ear. She told them to go eat and make themselves comfortable.

"Aye, Mrs. Diane, hope you didn't mind me bringing a couple of friends. They all wanted to come and pay their respects."

"Of course I don't mind. Where is Tiffany?"

"She supposed to met me here." He sighed while shaking his head in frustration. "I thought she would've beat me here."

"I hope you're hungry."

"Starving!" Jeffrey replied, holding his stomach. "I made sure I didn't eat nothing"

"Well good, because its plenty of food to eat. I'll fix you a plate. You want everything right?"

"Hold the pork!"

Diane laughed, "You and that Lamont a trip!" She would always tease LA about eating pork. "***Boy, I raised your ass off of pork. What the hell you talking about don't buy no more?***" She would always say.

Diane walked over to fix Jeffrey's plate, while he headed in the opposite direction, where uncle Lorenzo was entertaining his boys. He had everyone cracking up. When Lorenzo drank, he could put on a hell of a show.

"Yo Jeffrey, dude funny as shit!" Eco said as he joined the crowd of laughter.

"Say there... Nephew," the older man greeted Jeffrey with a pat on the shoulder. Lorenzo looked around to make sure his sisters weren't close by.

"Where the bud at?" The youngster laughed to no end while Lorenzo stood there trying to figure out what was so funny.

"Come on now, all y'all motherfuckers rolling together, one of you gotta have it. Put in the air!" Lorenzo kept at it.

"Here comes Diane," Jeffrey whispers.

Diane knew her brother like the back of her hand and could tell when he was up to no good. "Here you go sweetie, pork free." Diane eyed her brother suspiciously. "Is he bothering y'all?"

"Naw, he aight," everyone answered in sync.

"Thanks Mrs. Diane," Jeffrey said and proceeded to take a bite of the crispy piece of chicken.

"You welcome, baby. If y'all need anything else, I'll be at the grill." She began to walk off when Jeffrey stopped her. "What is it baby?"

"Uh………. Can we go to the tool shed? You know what us young-sters like to do."

She hesitated then smiled. "Go ahead boy. I'm only doing this be-cause it's Lamont's party and I know he used to smoke that shit. Close the door behind you. I don't wanna smell it."

Jeffrey rushes off like a little child. Lorenzo and the youngsters packs up in the shed, while Jeffrey and Eco post up outside and eat.

"Yo Jeff, look who done crashed the party. It's about to be on in this piece," Eco remarks as his eyes bulge at the sight of the two figures.

Jeffrey couldn't believe it. His appetite vanishes at first glance of Shonda and her mother. He and Shonda had been cool through the chaos, but he hadn't spoken to Shannon since she aired him out at Angie's funeral. His heart pounds as Shonda spots him and starts walking in his direction. Her mother stays back…. Thank God.

"I'm telling you right now Eco… If shorty pop slick out her mouth today, I'm gone let her ass have it!"

"Hi Eco…. Jeffrey, can I speak with you for a minute?" Wiping his hands on a napkin, Jeffrey reluctantly steps off with Shonda. Eco goes inside the shed to join the puff session. He opens the door and clouds of smoke smacks him dead in his face.

"Shonda, what's good? Give a nigga a hug girl, you know we family."

She hugs Jeffrey, and then glances over at her mother, standing alone, looking out of place. "She wants to talk to you Jeffrey."

"I don't know about that Shonda."

"Boy, come on." She takes his hand like a mother would do a child and leads him over. The three of them stand in a corner by themselves. Shannon and Jeffrey both eying one another, neither of them speaking.

Shannon takes a deep breath. "Jeffrey, I know you mad at me for the way I behaved at my daughter's funeral.... I was hurting baby." Jeffrey tries to cut her off, but she hold up her hand.

"Let me finish. I've been waiting to talk to you for a while now. I don't know what came over me.... All I know is... I lost my baby and you were the only person I could take it out on...." Another deep sigh and she says,

"I forgot about you losing your mother and everything else you've been going through since her death. I hated LA for what happened to my daughter.... I wished everything under the sun would happen to him. But when I saw his face on the news.... I read the papers on how he went after her killer and hunted him down. I realized that he really was a good person to do that. He really loved Angie." Tears fall down her face.

"Jeffrey.................................... Please forgive me."
When she finish talking, both Shonda and Jeffrey looks at one another surprised. Jeffrey takes Shannon into his arms, hugs her and says that neither LA nor Angie would be pleased with their behavior.

"Yeah, I forgive you." Jeffrey held her hand and told her that there was someone there he wanted her to meet. Diane and her sister, wondering who the strangers were, she grabs napkins from the table and wipes her hands.

"Mrs. Diane, this is Angie's mother, Shannon. Shannon, this is L A's mother, Diane." Jeffrey and Shonda steps back as the two women stand in an awkward silence for almost an entire minute. Their last encounter wasn't a pleasant one. Before when they had spoken, LA was still alive and Angie was dead. But now they were meeting under entirely different circumstances. Both had suffered the pain of losing a child.

"Hello Shannon?" Diane says finally and extends out her hand. Their hands connect and Shannon's reaction shocks everyone. Instead of a handshake, she delivers a heartfelt hug. Both women shared the same grief.

In an instant, the two were crying in each other's arms. A joyous moment it was. Everyone stood back, watching as the pair displayed their deepest emotions.

So caught up in the moment, Jeffrey didn't even realize Shonda holding one of his hands. Her eyes were saying something, but Jeffrey was too excited to pay attention. Diane and Shannon were now talking like the best of friends, while Pauline fixed their plates.

Jeffrey's crew was standing outside of the shed lifted, listening to Lorenzo crack jokes on everyone at the party, kids included. It was peace.... Everyone had settled their differences and was sitting back enjoying themselves as they celebrated the life of LA, Angie and all who weren't there.

CHAPTER 12

Finally things were starting to get better for Jeffrey. This was surely a day he'd never forget. Diane and Shannon's reunion was a definite sight to see. The two ladies had cried and talked, cried and talked, astounding all. It was a good thing Tiffany didn't show up and see how closely, Shonda clung to her man. Speaking of Tiffany, Jeffrey couldn't get his mind off her. She was supposed to have met him at Diane's, but never showed up.

He called her house several times and spoke with her mother, but even she hadn't heard a word from Tiffany. It was 12:00 am. Jeffrey and Eco, along with two carloads of youngsters behind them were headed to club '**Flavors**' in Petersburg. Tiffany misses the party and has the audacity to not even pick up the phone and at least let him know that she was okay.

Fuck her!" Jeffrey muttered furiously under his breath and inhaled the weed smoke. "Bitch probably out tricking!" Jeffrey was fuming but contained his anger. It even crossed his mind to go and look for her but he quickly decided against it."

The line was at the parking lot when Eco turned the corner on South Union St. "Man.. Man.. Man," Eco gawked at the three dime sexes tip toeing across the street in heels. "Damn, these hoes thick out here tonight." Jeffrey agreed. They were beautiful and curvy and everywhere Jeffrey looked. It was nearly impossible to find parking, but after a good 30 minutes of circling the block, they got lucky. As they exited the car, two Sedan Deville's pulled up beside them. The window rolled down and the passenger stuck his head out the window.

"Ain't no parking spaces," Mango yelled from the passenger seat. "We gone park on the street."

"Aight, will wait for y'all," Jeffrey yelled back while at the same time, lifting his ringing cell phone to his ear. "Yo," he spoke into the receiver....

What, you for real... How long ago this happen? Damn mane!! Do she got a bond? Aight bet, give me a minute, I'll be there."

Jeffrey hung up the phone and called out to Eco standing near a gold Honda with two chicks who were on their way to the club. He gave one of them a piece of paper, and then turned to see what Jeffrey wanted.

He throws up his arms. "What's wrong?"

"Tiffany ass locked up. She hardheaded as shit!!!"

"For what?" Eco looked at his friend puzzled.

"Remember the pounds I had left?" Eco shook his head. "I had it in the trunk of her car. I specifically told her ass before I left to take all the shit out!"

"Wow... Damn. So what the fuck you gone do? Fifteen pounds though. She got a bond?"

"I have no fucking clue...." Jeffrey stood there stunned. "My whole night is fucked!!!!!"

"Don't sweat it mane... Its weed, what the fuck you about to have a baby for nigga."

The news cast such a gloom over Jeffrey, that he was physically weak. He had a bad taste in his mouth. Jeffrey leaned on the front hood of the Cadillac, looked at Eco. "The burner was in there too mane. They got the smoke and the motherfucking heat!!!"

"**WHAT**! Goddamn playa!!"

"I got the worst fucking luck in the world." A few minutes past as they stand there discussing their latest obstacle. The boys walk up around this time, excited about getting their night started only to be shattered by Jeffrey's disappointment.

"May as well enjoy tonight," suggested Eco. "It could be a while before you see all this again. "His gold fronts glistened through a mischievous smile under the stark street lights. He pointed to a pair of Asian chicks walking by checking them out. The temptation was tremendous. Eco and the rest of the crew tried vigorously to convince Jeffrey to come inside the club to no avail.

Jeffrey was clearly ready to go. He opened the door and sat down in the passenger seat. Eco stared painfully down the block, filled with clutters of party goers and lovely, half dressed women. He couldn't believe that of all nights, Tiffany had to go and get herself locked up on this one.

"Damn you Tiff," he stated before getting into the car, cranking the engine and driving away.

The Ghost

CHAPTER 13

Down at the precinct, Detective Rasheed peered through a one way glass at the tough female, rethinking another approach to use on her, aware that she was far from a fool. Entering the interrogation room, the detective observed Tiffany for a few moments in silence. She had her head down on the table and it was obvious from the puffy eyes, that she'd been crying.

"How you doing?"

Tiffany sucked her teeth and rolled her eyes. If looks could kill, he would have drop dead on the spot.

"Do you know that you're facing Federal charges?" Detective Rasheed waited for her reply.

"Why am I still here?" Tiffany's eyes were full of hatred.

The detective got in her face. "You're still here because you are not telling us the truth!"

"Did you or did you not find the shit in my car?" Tiffany was tired and hadn't eaten in hours.

"Yes, all 15 pounds of marijuana were found in your car, along with the weapon, but we're not fools. We know who it belongs to and that person is definitely not you. I know you're a brave girl, but please don't be stupid. Is this guy worth doing years in the slammer and ruining your clean record? You take this charge and you're going to Federal prison, I can promise you that!" His words did nothing to her.

"Look, I ain't got shit else to say, I'm tired of talking to you."

"We know who it belongs to!"
"Just do whatever you gone do with me!!"

All Tiffany could hear was Jeffrey's words, 'Make sure you put that shit up before you drive out to the party.'

"How could I be so fucking dumb???" She questioned herself. "So, you're not going to talk to me?"

"Nope," replied Tiffany.

" I promise.... You'll wish you had!"

CHAPTER 14

It was Monday morning when Tiffany's mother, Gladys and Jeffrey strolled into the courtroom and sat down on the second row. Because she was arrested over the weekend, she couldn't get a bond until today. Gladys had already made arrangements with the bails bondsman. Now, they were waiting on the judge to set the amount.

Tiffany appeared restless when she entered the courtroom. Her eyes were puffy from crying and her hair was in a ponytail. Her mother gave her an encouraging smile as the Deputy took her in front of the judge. She blushed horribly as Jeffrey blew a kiss and winked his eye at her. Tiffany knew her mother would be there, but with Jeffrey running the streets and all, she just didn't expect him to step foot inside a courtroom.

Jeffrey notices the prosecutor and a suited detective giving him a hard stare and every so often, one would nod their head in his direction. He plays it cool and whispers in Gladys ear. After the judge set a $10,000 bail, Jeffrey quietly raise to a stance and proceeds to walk smoothly towards the exit but is intercepted by two plain clothed DEA agents. They cut him off right before he could get out of the door completely. Badges were flashed and the agents identified him before placing him under arrest. People watched in awe as the two agents escorted the young man from the courtroom.

"Why are you arresting me?" Jeffrey turns to one agent and asks while the other cuff him from behind.

Gladys comes rushing out. "What's going on? Why are you arresting him?!!!"

"Ma'am, you need to step back and mind your business!"

"Get in touch with Diane for me!" Jeffrey hollers out as they ushers him quickly through a doorway that leads to the stairs. Gladys stands outside of the courtroom confused. She reenters the room, but Tiffany has gone.

The bondsmen approaches her along with two agents and Detective Strickland. "Your daughter is going to be charged with obstruction of justice," said the hard face detective.

"For what?" The concerned mother asked.

"She's hindering our investigation by claiming ownership of a gun and drugs known to belong to Mr. Owen's."

Gladys stood there tongue tied. "Will Tiffany be released?"

"Sure," replied the bondsman. "Will have her out in the next hour or so."

"Where'd they take Jeffrey, and what is he charged with?"

"He's going down to headquarters," Rasheed replied evasively. He was the second detective.

"Ma'am, we tried to work with your daughter. We know everything belongs to her boyfriend. I told her she'd regret not talking to me. Now she's facing 18 months for the obstruction charge alone, not to mention the gun and marijuana. Those are Federal charges. Have you heard of "**Project Exile?**" Strickland asked.

"No," Gladys replied.

"It's a new program that targets illegal guns," Rasheed interjected. "With her clean slate, she's still looking at a minimum of 2 1/2 years. Luckily, she has no priors or she'd be doing five."

The officer had scared the poor woman to death. She left out the

Federal Court building in tears, following the bondsman to the city jail to bond her daughter out.

The Ghost

CHAPTER 15

Detective enters the interrogation room. "How you doing, Mr. Owen's? Want anything, soda, pizza, a cigarette.... To go home???"

Jeffrey sat stone faced in the interrogation room at the DEA headquarters. He glared at the over friendly agent. "What I want is your name and why the hell you got me here!"

"Easy, easy buddy. All is not what it seems, this can go so smoothly, you'll never know you were here. I'm agent Strickland, you smoke?"

"What can go smooth?" I ain't did shit! Why am I here?" Jeffrey fumed.

"Well, I see you wanna get right down to business, so let's not waste anymore time." Strickland pulls out a chair from under the table, and takes a seat across from Jeffrey.

"You're pretty tight with Percy Miller, a guy our department has wanted for a long time. Consider this a favor for a favor. You give us a detailed statement, describing the times in the last couple years or so that you've purchased drugs from him, Tiffany walks. Huh, what do you say Jeff? A half an hour of your time and you two love birds are back in the love nest, reunited."

Jeffrey barely let the man finish his statement before he responded.

"Kiss my ass! Mane, what the fuck is up? We ain't got no business, so I'm ready to step!"

Rasheed enters the room just in time to hear Jeffrey invite the detective to kiss his backside. "Ouch," agent Rasheed mouths.

Strickland continues. "Kiss your ass." The agent replies softly.

"Mr. Owen's, that's not exactly my idea of a resolution. I'll give you some time to rethink this." Strickland got up and made his way toward the door.

"Mane, you can't hold me withou-" the slamming of the door silenced Jeffrey's words. Strickland joined the detective outside, leaving him in complete solitude. Jeffrey sat there in an eerie silence for close to an hour before the sound of the doorknob clicking, alerted him to the agents return. Strickland took his place back across from Jeffrey.

"So Jeffrey, what have you been thinking about my man?" The approach was the same but the tone was different. Jeffrey lifts up his head and focuses his eyes on the face.

"Yo, I been thinking about y'all letting me the fuck go. Real talk, why y'all holding me?"

"Well, I see kindness is not your cup of tea, so we'll try this another way." The detective turned his back to Jeffrey, walking until he was almost touching the opposite wall. He stopped and paused for a few seconds as a deadly silence overtook the room. Then, in one fluid motion, he spun around, eyes locked on the youngster.

"Remember when you were 13 Jeffrey?"

"What?"

"13, young and bright, full of potential."

"Cut the shit mane, I'm ready to-"

"A good kid for the most part, rarely into trouble.................... That is, of course, other than that one time your boy Black had you drunk as a skunk behind Oak Grove Elementary and your mom, God rest her soul, got a call from the County saying her son had been picked up for Trespassing.

"What the hell you getting at?"

Strickland studied the menacing look on Jeffrey's face, detecting a hint of concern.... Possibly fear. He let his words sink in for a moment, then spoke slowly, "the Glock Jeffrey.............. Your prints came back clear as day on the clip. In so many words.........You bought the beef."

Jeffrey's face crumbles at the statement. Strickland gives him a few seconds to come to grips with reality. He could recall the arrest like it was yesterday. And the giant police officer that took his prints... God he was so young then. Seizing what the detective considered to be an opportunity, he pulled out a chair next to Jeffrey and sat down. His tone changed to that of a caring cop.

"Look man, let's make this go away. You've got too much going for you to be sitting in some jail cell rotting a way, while your sisters need you. It's like this, Jeff. You give us 30 minutes of your time and none of this shit ever happen... But if you buck.... Be Billy bad ass.... Both you and Tiffany are going up the road for a long time. So bro, what's it gonna be?"

Strickland turns to face Jeffrey, whose face is now buried in his hands. He taps him lightly on the shoulder, hoping to provoke a response. Jeffrey's head snaps back, revealing an emotionless stare, ***"take me to book-ing."***

The Ghost

CHAPTER 16

Silence comes over the entire G2 tier when Big Lee approaches the steel bars like a hungry lion with a meal before him, waiting for the gate to open. The crap game that had been in full swing only moments earlier, ended abruptly. It was his routine heist. Convicts cleared out, brothers hid their goodies, knowing that the big man was coming through to collect. Guy's moved out the way as the giant walked through with his massive arms, glowing and extremely intimidating. There were rumors of him beating a man to death with his bare hands, so no one ever challenged him.

Three poker games were also in full swing upon his arrival. But by the time he walked through with his scary ice grill, all the tables were bare. The deputies were terrified of him and lived to see him give his fellow prisoners a hard time. Big Lee was the only cat in the jail that got to have contact visits. He was also allowed to roam all over the facility whenever he wanted. Whether it be drugs to support his dope habit or canteen, deputies would escort him to wherever he needed to go.

His eyes glittered dangerously around the room at all his inmate prey .

"Where do Prince sleep at?" Everyone answers at once, some even pointed to the O G's cell.

"I'm going to holler at my man. When I get back, y'all niggas make sure my shit on the table." No one said a word.

Prince was on his bed reading a Spielberg's novel when he felt eyes

69

peering down on him. The minute he saw who it was, Prince shook his head and grinned.

"Big homey, what brings you to my neck of the woods." Prince glanced over the giant's shoulder just in time to see one of the prisoners, lugging a huge pillow case, stacked with canteen over to a card table. "I see you still making yo rounds."

"Well a nigga gotta survive," Big Lee replied. "I see you still bidding off those books."

The two had spent a few years together in James River.

"Yeah, I don't see no other way to do it," he replied glumly.

"You know a young kid named Jeffrey?"

"What about him?" Prince asked sharply.

"The nigga in the bullpen right now. He told me to tell you to holler at him."

Prince shook his head and sighed. "What the fuck is this nigga doing in here??" Prince was clearly bothered by this. "I told the young nigga to chill the fuck out!"

"What up though, you good?" Big Lee asked, taking a seat next to Prince.

"I need to talk to him right away," Prince muttered to no one in particular. He didn't like it. What the fuck was going on?! He rubbed his temples in pure frustration.

"Say no more...." Big Lee says and get up. "Follow me."

"Where to?"

"You say you need to talk to the young nigga, right? I run this shit in here, you know that!"

Without questions, Prince slips his shrubs on and follows the mon-

70

ster of a man out of his prison cell. On their way to the front, Big Lee stops at the table, picks up a huge pillowcase stuffed with canteen. Big Lee hadn't changed a bit, still roughing stuff off. He called Prince's name and signaled for him to follow. The O G moved swiftly as the Deputy lead the way.

'Bad man!' Prince thought as he watched the big homey order around the Jail Deputies.

They came to a complete stop at the end of the corridor where the new arrivals had just come in from court. Prince scanned the narrow hall way and took a step back upon hearing the crack of the steel gates opening. Big Lee hesitates and taps the Deputy's shoulder on their way in.

"Yo Dept, let my man get a couple minutes of privacy. The young nigga like his son, it won't take long."

They never denied him. "Alright Miller, make it quick, I gotta get you all back before chow time. Cell six!" The white Deputy calls out.

Prince takes off before the officer can say another word. Jeffrey was already posted up at the bars when the O G walked up.

"I don't have a lot of time! Damn man, what the hell you doing back here?"

"Man, it's some straight bullshit. You remember my girl Tiffany, right?"

Prince nodded his head and waited for him to continue. "The police stopped her, searched the car and found 15 pounds of bud and a burner."

"And it was yours," O G replied somberly while shaking his head in utter disappoint. "God damn young nigga, what happen to chilling the fuck out??"

Jeffrey lowered his head in shame against the cold steel bars.

"Prince, it ain't even about the stuff they found. They crossed shorty up only to get to me."

"What do you mean? Why the fuck would they want you?"

"You don't know nigga.... These motherfuckers drilled me for two hours, trying to get me to tell them that

I got work from you. They said all I had to do is say yes and they would drop my charges and Tiffany's charges."

"Is that right".... Prince stares across at Jeffrey, stroking his goatee. *It's exactly what he thought it was.* Law enforcement wanted his head on a platter. The O G peeks back at the Deputy, then he turns to Jeffrey. "So what did you tell them pig motherfuckers??!!"

"**To kiss my black ass.... Straight like that!**" They were standing face to face now and Prince found himself trying to study the youngster for any sign of betrayal. Prince eyed him without blinking once because he knew how hard pressed the Feds were after him. So many bad thoughts. Like what if he never made it out? They couldn't get the **Juice Crew** to roll over on him 10 years ago. Black's plot didn't work and LA was dead. If this was how it was going down, he wanted to know personally if or not Jeffrey intended to burn him. It didn't matter that he never did business with Jeffrey, if they wanted their man, they would go through great lengths to get him... **Even lie..**

"So that's your word..."

"On my mama my nigga." Jeffrey didn't bat an eye.

A smile stretches wide across Prince's lips. "I believe you bro. So what now? Do you think they got a case?"

Jeffrey nods his head sadly. "They caught Tiff red handed. I told her to take the shit out the car. They shipping me to a Regional Jail in the morning."

"Time's up!" Announced the Deputy.

"Alright," Prince said. "Why they shipping you though?"

"They talking about I got fed charges."

"Oh yeah, they probably got you under that Exile shit."

"I can't let shorty take that weapons beef, Prince."

"I understand exactly what you mean. The most you'd do is three years."

Jeffrey took a deep breath, shook his head in despair. *"I can't win for losing."*

The Ghost

CHAPTER 17

Diane retained Peter Jennings as Counsel for Jeffrey. He did everything he could for him, but all the skills in the world didn't mean jack in Federal court. Even after cooperating with Tiffany's attorney, he still couldn't find one loophole in the case. The officers had ***probable cause*** to search her car. She didn't have her license present, not to mention the open Heineken beer bottle sitting directly in the cup holder as if she had a permit to drink and drive.

Mr. Jennings told Jeffrey he was sitting between a rock and a hard place. The Feds were already mad at him for not crossing Prince, so they played hardball and made up bogus excuses as to why he shouldn't be released on bail pending his court date. The judge went along with the prosecutor. Diane was right there at court, even stood up and spoke to the judge about releasing him in her custody, but it didn't work.

Tiffany's confession certainly didn't help matters. Had not Jeffrey's prints been on the gun, he would never have been charged. There was only one option, plea out to the gun and marijuana, so Tiffany's charges would be dropped. The prosecutor agreed to dismiss the obstruction charge as well, but only if Jeffrey took the weight.

Prince had been home for two weeks. His case was dismissed without his presence. Wanda and little Pernell were waiting outside the jail to welcome him home. After he situated himself, he had Jeffrey's belongings transferred from his apartment into storage. Prince then drove 45 minutes to Piedmont Regional Jail to visit him. The pain was evident in Jeffrey's eye's and Prince couldn't help but feel compassion for him. Prince did his best to reassure him that his sisters would be taken care of.

Everything was happening so fast. Jeffrey was just on the streets, trying to build a bankroll, now here he was sitting inside a Regional Jail ready to be transported to a Federal Prison.

"Damn, **shit was all good just a week ago,**" thought Jeffrey as he relaxed on the top bunk, observing everyone. Blacks of course were the majority. His first time ever being locked up, Jeffrey was devastated and felt lost among all the unfamiliar faces. He couldn't eat nor could he sleep. Some brothers even approached him and asked if he was okay. Others stood back, whispering amongst one another.

"*He just coming in... Look at him, he sick as shit!*"

"*Bet his ass be eating by the end of the week,*" Bubba joked to the guys next to him as they watched Jeffrey decline his meal.

The youngster was miserable and everybody could see it. He just couldn't believe that after all he'd been through, things could actually get worse. He was living a nightmare. Every morning, he awakened to disgust, recognizing the grim reality. Jeffrey tried to convince himself that it was all for a reason. His life had changed dramatically. And his faith in God left with the death of his mother. An unknown force was driving everyone he cared about away from him.

Although her apology made him feel no better, Tiffany did make an attempt. Jeffrey jumped down from the bunk and put on his brand new Air force ones. In Piedmont, inmates could wear shoes from the streets and even order food from outside restaurants. Jeffrey's stomach growled as the aroma from KFC filled his nose.

"Damn, gotta get my paper straight. Aye slim, do you have some paper and pencil?"

"Sure buddy." The full bearded white guy replied as he walked off toward his bunk.

The guy grabbed a notebook, ripped a few sheets off and handed them to Jeffrey. "Here's a ink pen buddy. Lost the pencil I had."

"Thanks man, I'll make sure you get this back," replied Jeffrey.

"No, keep it my brother. I got plenty." He held his hand out, "my names Bill, what's yours?"

Jeffrey told him his name as they shook hands and then parted ways. He walked over to an empty folding chair and sat..... He hesitated for a moment then proceeded to write:

My mind is full of painful memories. My countenance reveals the life struggle I was dealt. My family is all I have to live for. Who do I have to love me mom without you around anymore?
My friends are nonexistent, either dead or in prison and my sisters.... Snatched away!!!! Both my mother and father.... Dead!!!!! Tears from my pain run as deep as the Nile.... I am fucked up inside, thinking, if I had a burner right now, I'd put a bullet in my own head.
I know that you didn't raise me to be weak, but mama I need you now more than ever before in my life! Memories of the past flash through my head. And the pain is obvious from the tears that I shed. Keep asking, why me? What the fuck I do wrong? Guess I was weak, when I should have been strong....

"Count time! Count time!"

The Ghost

CHAPTER 18

It took Diane a minute to recognize the dismantled figure standing before her. She even squinted her eyes in an effort to place the face. Two swollen eyes and walking with a cane, Black looked horrible. He was like a son to her and it stung the very core of her heart seeing him in such a condition. Picking up the phone, she watched him fumble in pain, trying to put the receiver to his ear.

"Boy, what the hell done happen to you? God, look at you! Who did this shit?"

Black shook his head and named his assailants.

"Why would they do this to you?" She stared at him through a set of sympathetic eyes as he painfully tried to reply. Black manages to grin. It had been a while since anyone had extended any love his way. "It's a long story," was all Black would say. "How you doing?" What's up with Jeffrey?"

"Don't try to change the subject. I'm waiting on an answer! Them motherfuckers beat you down and I'll get a lawyer! They ain't got no business putting their hands on you!" Diane was livid. He ran the whole story down about how he found out about L A's death. He expressed deep hurt and Diane could feel pain leak out of every word that he spoke. He thanked her continuously for visiting him. For a minute, he started to think no one cared. She doubled over in laughter hearing Black's detailed description of how he blanked out on Detective Daniel's. Then they both shared a tear when he confessed that his intention was to make the detective kill him.

He nearly slipped up and mention the deceased picture of her son shown to him by the detectives. But he didn't. They laughed and joked about the old days, reminiscing about the times when life was much more pleasant. Diane began to describe the event she'd thrown for her son. Black grew excited listening to her boast about how crowded the party was. She told him about Jeffrey and all the guys who crashed the party. He was relieved to hear she'd respected L A's wishes. They discussed Jeffrey's ordeal, and how happy he was not to be facing that much time. Naturally, Black looked a bit uncomfortable at the mention of Prince's name and plans to get custody of Erica and Britney. He felt terrible about rolling over on the O G and wished that he could take it all back.

"Do you think Prince will be able to get them?"

"I don't see why not," Diane replied with confidence. He seemed like he was serious about it." "So, how you really doing? What's going on with your case? You got a lawyer, need any money?"

"Yeah, I could use some money"

"I'll leave it at the end of the visit. What about your case, when you coming home?"

Black took in a deep breath as his eyes suddenly turned watery. He looked up at the only mother he'd ever known, choking back tears. He didn't want to cry in front of her.... Hadn't even had a chance to process his new reality. But if there was one thing he was certain of, that would be, "*I'm never coming home, ma*."

Diane felt terrible and pressed her hand against the Plexiglas in a gesture of affection. She wished that she could hold him. She thought as she stared through the glass at Black, 'if it wasn't violent crimes claiming the lives of so many youth, it was **penal systems**.' Not even six months had passed since she buried her only son.... And now she was about to lose another child who was just like a son... *To prison... "God, help us,"* she cried out in prayer!

CHAPTER 19

Wanda and Pernell had been clinging to Prince's side ever since his release, even when he traveled out of town on business. A great amount of his income was generated from the various properties he owned. In prison, he studied real estate, learning everything there was to know about it. Four out of seven units he currently own were being renovated. He'd buy run down pads, fix them up and make a killing.

Prince had made a fortune off the restaurant as well, especially the Shock Bar in Atlanta. It had three floors, and attracted all the big time stars. Everybody who was anybody hung out there, netting Prince over $1 million last year alone. So far, there hadn't been any trouble, and everyone respected his place.

Wanda was overwhelmed when Prince led her to the V. I. P. section of his club. It absolutely blew her mind to walk in a room and rub shoulders with some of her favorite rappers and entertainers. Jermaine Dupree, Outkast and the whole Dungeon family were lounging in VIP, surrounded by some of the most beautiful women Wanda had ever laid eyes on. She had no idea her man was this large. He introduced her to everybody, even the people who ran the club for him. She was speechless when Evander Holyfield knocked on their front door.

Wanda was unhappy to say the least, when it was time to return to Richmond. She practically begged Prince to stay in Atlanta. Even though he'd promise to pack up and leave Richmond once his case was over, something held him back. Erica and Britney were constantly on his mind. For some reason, he felt responsible for them. He could still see their faces when he stood there with Mrs. Anderson, discussing the possibility of seeking custody. The caseworker was very nice and down-to-earth, seeming as though she really wanted the best for the girls.

"All they need is for someone to love and provide a stable environment for them," the caseworker informed him. She was stunned when she pulled in front of the beautiful house Prince was providing to accommodate the children. "I'll do everything I can to get you these kids," she told the couple.

"Although it may take up to six months to get a court date, I assure you that my recommendations will go a long way with the judge."

CHAPTER 20

The movers had just loaded the last piece of Wanda's furniture into the truck. It had been a long time since Prince had visited his old projects. Grey Stone had definitely changed since his days on the block. He sat down on the stoop and observed the little shorties running down cars and holding down the block. Brought back old memories. Prince hated not being able to communicate with any of his boys.

Up the block, he spotted several kids at the corner playing. Two were squared off in the streets, slap boxing while the other stood on the curb, laughing and goofing around. In another two or three years, those same kids would be running the block, possibly selling crack, history repeating itself. The older brothers would either be dead or in prison, giving the younger generation a opportunity for a piece of the pie. The cycle went on and on, *it was all in the elite's plan.*

This was the same housing project that had made him a rich man. What else could he do? He was already a strong force in the community, donating thousands of dollars to the Boys and Girls Club. Every year, he purchased new equipment for the football teams, but still his conscience plagued him.

"Damn," he muttered, watching one of the kids yell out five-0, alerting the dealers of the police's presence. The once crowded block was now empty as the squad car drove by slowly. Geraldine, a third generation crack head in her late 50s, with streaks of gray hair, saw the O G and went berserk. Prince smiled as the woman hurriedly made her way toward him. It had been years since he'd last saw her. She was a proud junkie. Geraldine could've been a millionaire by now if she'd saved all the money and coke that slipped through her hands.

"If it ain't the smartest hustler I ever known," Geraldine screamed, "boy, where you been??? You better come and give me a hug!!!"

Prince squeezed the frail woman tightly. "Woman, what the hell you been doing all this time?"

"You know, ol' Geraldine still working these streets, hustling the best way I know how... Damn boy, it sho is good to see you!" Stepping back, she stared Prince up and down. "You still looking good too." She turned and faced the street. "Are you driving that car?" The Range Rover glistened.

"Girl, you know how I do. So, how you been? I see you still out here giving them hell." They shared a laugh and caught up on old times.

"You know these young boys out here today don't do nothing right. It ain't like it used to be when you was out here. These fools don't got a clue how to get money. I tried to give them game, but they look at you crazy. They think I's just a little old dumb crack head. Think they know it all."

"These dudes got you twisted baby."

"You got that right Prince. Ever since that LA and Black left, these niggas done lost their minds. I sure am glad you left this shit alone because this ain't about nothing out here."

The movers had just finished. Wanda locked the door to her vacant apartment and joined Prince and Geraldine on the steps. "You know I'm going to beat you girl!" Geraldine said playfully. "Ain't nobody tell you to go running off and don't tell nobody."

The two women had an awkward exchange. Geraldine secretly envied Wanda. '*If only she knew what she had,*' thought Geraldine. Prince was every woman's dream. Tall, dark and handsome, for many years, Geraldine fantasized about Prince.

"I'll be waiting in the car. You know we got to meet the people at the house." Wanda walks off. "Bye Geraldine".

"Alright now girl."

"I'm coming," Prince holler and turn to face his old and dear friend, who'd given him much game coming up. "I'm glad I ran in to you. Take your time out here baby girl." Another hug. "You need anything?"

"I doubt if you got what I want. Damn boy, I miss that stuff you used to have."
"Can't help you in that department, I gotta couple of bills for you, though." Prince reaches in his pocket and gives her a crispy hundred.

"All these years done passed and still, ain't nobody out here that can fill your shoes."

"I gotta go." Prince walks to his truck, turning for one last time to look at his old friend before opening the door. Prince shook his head, watching the woman flutter across the street to buy a fix with the money he'd just given her. In the car, he rested his head back against the cushion, staring in the rear view at Geraldine and the children on the corner.

"What's wrong?" Asked Wanda driving off.

"I hate this shit!" He states and sighs bitterly.

"What do you mean, what do you hate?"

"Look at them knuckleheads right there."

Wanda directs her attention to the boys playing at the top of the corner as she drives slowly pass them.

"Okay, so what about them?"

"What do you see?"

Wanda appears to be puzzled, laughing innocently. "I see kids having fun Prince."

The O G laughs at his naive counterpart. "They ain't playing woman. Those ghetto bastards are posted up, watching for the police. I'll bet money that none of them got fathers at home."

The car becomes silent and she turns to Prince saying, "babe, I know how you feel, but damn boo, you can't do but so much. Nobody in this city do more for these children than you. You support all the clubs and give away money like you're Santa Clause."

Wanda rubbed her soft palm against his neck to ease his tension. "Look at me."

He faces her and their lips meet for a passionate kiss as they pause momentarily at a stop sign.

"You can't save everybody, it's impossible."

Studying her statement for a moment, Prince hesitates while at the same time, gazing out of the rear view window. "Maybe you right." Range

Rover speeds up, images of Grey Stone in the near distance.

CHAPTER 21

Time seemed to have come to a halt for Tiffany ever since her man went on lock. She was in tears every time she left Piedmont Jail. Only a few months passed since Jeffrey's arrests, and already she was miserable. "Two years ain't that long," she encouraged herself. Although he claimed not to be mad at her, she knew deep down inside he despised her. Some visits, Jeffrey oftentimes wouldn't even look her in the eyes.

Yet and still, she tried her hardest to make up for her mistakes. Every weekend, she made it up to visit him in jail, driving 45 minutes just to visit him for 30 minutes. Whenever he called, she was right there to answer. Jeffrey had stolen her heart and she was determined to prove to him that her love was true. Her friends thought that she'd lost her mind. Tiffany had barely left her apartment since Jeffrey's arrest. And recently, she began to receive constant calls from friends with so called dirt on Jeffrey. The regular, he said, she said madness. Tiffany knew this would happen. Now that Jeffrey wasn't there to defend himself, people all of a sudden wanted to start gossiping. She didn't buy in to it.

Ayesha, her girlfriend didn't let up, continuing to poison Tiffany's mind with the,(a*ll men ain't shit nonsense.*) "Girl, you need to get your butt out of this apartment and have some fun. I don't know why you out here trying to be faithful. He wouldn't be! Let your ass go to jail, I bet he be fucking everything he see!"

"Girl, why don't you just shut up, dang! You don't know what the hell you talking about."

"Come on y'all, you know the club will be packed." Added Trina as she looked at her two best friends."

"I can't go out with you tonight. Jeffrey is suppose to be calling at

10:30." Ayesha looks at Tiffany, then at Trina and they giggle at Tiffany's statement.

"Next week, I promise." Tiffany assured them.

"Alright, but I told you Rakee been asking about you." Ayesha teased. "He's gonna be there tonight too. You saw the Lexus that nigga pushing?"

"Oh, that bitch is bad!" Trina cosigns. "I swear, when the nigga pulled up beside me at the stop light the other day, my pussy started jumping!"

Everyone laughs. "Damn you a freak." Tiffany teases.

"Please girl, come out with us tonight!" Begs Ayesha.

"I can't, he gonna call in 30 minutes. The phones cut off at 11 o'clock, you know that."

"Okay, so what do you want me to tell Rakee? I am sick of him asking me about you. Why don't I just give him your number."

"You better not give my number out! Besides, he knows I got a boy friend."

Ayesha eyes Tiffany and says, "Where the fuck he at?"

"Locked up," Trina adds. "Girl, you need some dick bad because you are too damn grouchy." Trina drifts into deep thought. "Um, and I hear that he's strapped with a MONSTER!!" *Laughs.*

"Why don't you just fuck him then!!" Tiffany barks back at her friends, becoming irritated by the pressure.

"We'll call you tomorrow to let you know about the good time you missed. Tell Jeffrey we said hi."

After locking the door behind them, Tiffany stretches out on her couch, relaxing as she waits for the love of her life to call.

The Ghost

CHAPTER 22

Dear Jeffrey,

How are you doing? Fine I hope. As for us, Brittany and I are good. We just left from seeing you. The visits are so short, so I thought I could write you a letter. Brittany is so smart. It seems like every day she does or says something that amazes me. We miss you a whole lot. I can't wait until we are back together as a family again. Britney talks about you all the time.

There's no doubt she misses her brother. I think she's starting to understand that mama ain't coming back. I try to be as honest as possible to her. Lying will only make matters worse. Jeffrey, I know you're happy to see us but how come you never smile? I know you've been through a lot and you probably feel like there's nothing to smile about. At least things are starting to get better for us like you said.

Prince is very nice. He comes by and checks on us all the time. Every other weekend, he takes us somewhere. He brought us clothes too. And the house we gonna live in is nice. We have our own rooms and a huge backyard. I just can't wait to move in.

Mrs. Anderson spoke with the judge and we now have a court date. I'm so tired of this place. I feel like I'm locked up or something. Wanda's real cool too. She calls us a lot. She says we are going to Disney World this weekend and Britney can't wait. I don't hear from Tiffany much.... She used to call when you first got locked up. Jeffrey, do you ever think about mama? I do.... All the time. I miss her so much. It's still hard to believe she's gone. I guess life goes on, right? Thank God you don't have a lot of time left to do. Hold your head up and smile sometimes. At least you still got life and of course, you got us. Gotta go, make sure you write back.

Love, Erica

A huge smile covers Jeffrey's face as he folds up Erica's letter, neatly placing it back inside its envelope. Overwhelmed with relief, just the thought of this rainstorm being over excited him. His sisters were happy. *'Five months from now, they'd be in their own house...Yes! I do got a lot to smile about.'* He loved reading letters from his sister. She always lifted his spirits up.

Tiffany was another blessing. The two of them talked on the phone every day, their relationship growing closer as time passed. He even started writing her love poems. She enjoyed reading them and even encouraged Jeffrey to write her at least one a week. He knew that his pen game was tight when he read one over the phone that brought her to tears.

Jeffrey had been sentence and was now waiting to be transferred to federal prison. He prayed to be shipped as close to home as possible, especially after hearing stories of how the Feds shipped prisoners all over the country. He adapted to the county jail life quickly. It surprised him to see everyone from his home town sticking together while on the streets, they'd bash each other's head in on sight.

In his housing unit, there were at least 8 to 10 guys from the city. Jeffrey wasn't too crazy about dealing with those who weren't from his set, particularly cats across town. It was said that Piedmont was the best place to do time, especially considering it provided inmates with lots of other high priced items that other facilities didn't provide. Mrs. Wright, who inmates referred to as (**Big Bertha**) ran the canteen department, making a killing, particularly from federal prisoners who was still connected to the streets. KFC, Chinese and Pizza Hut, were the three choices they had to select from. Whatever the restaurant charged, Mrs. Wright taxed the prisoners nearly double.

On the canteen list, she sold cassette players and even brought in all the latest Hip hop music from the streets. Mrs. Wright knew exactly what type of music to get. Between Jeffrey and his eight **Rich Town** buddies, the mob had all the latest music. On Fridays, they sat at their table with buckets of chicken, pizza and Chinese food, feasting amongst each other while the others inside the jail watched. Most of the prisoners lived right in Farm ville, a town so small that some inmates had family members working right at the facility.

For Jeffrey and his city boys to call home, the cost was $10 per call. Every week, he had Tiffany sending him hundreds of dollars. It was funny how going to prison could actually bring a man closer to his woman. He damn sure wasn't writing her poetry on the streets. Jeffrey was the first person on the phone when they turned on at 6 am and the last on the phone at night when they cut off.

It was 11:05. After hanging up the phone, Jeffrey walked over to his bunk and grabbed his radio. In another 10 minutes, the shifts would change and new officers would be coming on. Deputy Ferguson worked the night shift, the coolest African American officer in the facility. The inmates eagerly awaited his arrival. And although it was against the policy, he would come around every night with a list of people who were either going to court or getting transferred the following morning.

While the Deputies came through, shining flashlights and counting the men as if they were cattle, Jeffrey laid back on his bunk trying to relax, arms crossed behind his head with his earphones blasting, 'All eyes on me.' The tune's had him so zoned out, he didn't even realize count had cleared before his homeboy, Fat man came running over, excited and startling the hell out of him.

"What's up?" Asked Jeffrey.

"Our name on the list!! I saw it with my own eyes my nigga!!"

"For real," Jeffrey was elated. "Nigga, don't be playing games." Jeffrey jumped out of the bed.

"On everything I love my nigga. I wouldn't play around with you like that."

The two gave each other high fives and joined the rest of the guys. No one would get any sleep tonight. Whenever a friend left, they'd stay up half the night reminiscing, talking about what they planned to do once they got to prison. They were just happy to be leaving the jail.

Jeffrey would have to miss that party, at least until he finished the letter he was about to write. Notebook in hand, he strolled over to the empty table filled with excitement. Every night, he had been praying that his name would be on that list. All types of thoughts ran through his head. It had been almost 4 months since he'd hugged or kissed Tiffany.

"Damn," he thought. "*Can't wait to squeeze that soft ass! Might even get some pussy*." That brought a huge smile to his lips.

Everybody said that federal prison was supposedly the best place to do time ..... Guys got high and lived comfortable. Jeffrey just didn't get how prison should be considered by some to be sweet when he hated every day of his pathetic existence. Jeffrey put pen to paper.

Dear Erica,

What up girl? Nothing much here. Same shit, different day. Received your letter a couple days ago and I was glad to hear that everything is finally coming together. Oh, they are shipping me in the morning! I am happy as shit!! Tired of this jail. I dun spent over three grand in this bitch. Anyway, call Tiffany and let everybody else know too. Damn, I hope they don't send a nigga too far. Kiss Britney for me and give her my love.

I felt you on what you spoke about in your letter. About how I never smile. Sometimes I do feel like I don't got nothing to smile about. It's hard for me at times. It's been a minute since I felt I had a reason to smile and when I do try, it feels out of place. Like it don't belong there or something. I smile when I read your letters. Yeah, Prince told me about the house he had for y'all. That's my partner fasho. I'm glad he's holding us down for real. He said he would look out for us, though. But I wonder about that sometimes.... Can't wait until we get back together again. I never dream of mama, but I think about her all day sometimes. Take care sis, I just wanted to holla at you and let you know I won't be here tomorrow. I'll call or write whenever I get to where I'm going.

Love Ya'll Jeffrey

CHAPTER 23

The judge sentence Black to double life+40 years to serve for his part in the triple murders. Where was the logic in sentencing a man to two life sentences? Was he going to do one life, die then come back and do the other sentence?? He stood there beside his attorney motionless. Diane sat directly behind him on the second row, sobbing quietly. When the Deputy grabbed his arm, Black hesitated to turn and face Diane. After flashing her his best smile, he turned around and shot the two detectives a menacing glare as they sat, grinning directly behind the prosecutor.

In the months to follow, Black slowly started to deteriorate. The streets showed him no love. Before he received his sentence, a couple of the females he used to fool with, would stay in touch but as soon as they found out he had a life sentence, they started hanging up in his face. Some even blocked his calls. Many condemned Black on the strength of what he tried to do to Prince. Snitching was definitely not allowed on the streets of Richmond. Cats were dying every day because the word was put out that they were on a **snake mission**. Black was a firm believer in(**snitches get stitches**). On the Avenue, he regulated the block like a gorilla and in his words, *'a snitch was the worst thing a person could be.'*

When the pressure from the Feds came at him, threatening him with time, he found out just how strong he really was. Black could in fact be broken. At night, he would pray for death to come and end his misery. It was hard to go on, especially when no one loved him. He gave up on talking to anyone from the Avenue, except for Tiffany of course. She accepted his calls from time to time and kept him posted on Jeffrey's status. He moved around slowly, his broken ribs taking time to heal. His right eye had a permanent lump underneath it and one could easily tell that he was going ball. Black had a full beard, similar to the brothers around him at USP Marion. There were no short timers. Everyone in his unit was doing life, with the exception of a few with 40 and 50 years. Down 23 hours a day.

The Ghost

All they did was talk about the distant streets, reflecting back over their lives, trading war stories. There were guys who even bragged to one another about how they killed their victims. And the stories were the wackiest.

A white cat by the name of Richard was arrested along with his girlfriend. The story had made national news and ran for months on the ID channel. Inmates named the couple Bonnie and Clyde. The only difference was, he was a crack fiend who was pussy whipped. Supposedly, one night he was in the house somewhere in Blackstone Virginia, smoking crack with two black women and a white girl. He told how the three women sat there smoking up all his drugs and didn't want to give up the goods.

"All I wanted was some pussy, you know what I mean fellas?" The crowd nods, waiting for him to continue. "I was mad! I whipped out my 357 Magnum. Man, I swear them bitches pissed there panties. The black chick came up, told me she'd give me any thing I wanted." As he described how well built the sister was, prisoners laughed to no end at his southern accent. "We went in the room and Lord, the Bitch was a stallion!"

"Will you just get on with the story!" One of the listeners yells from the back.

"Anyways, before I could get my dick in her good, my goddamn girlfriend bust in the door and raise holy hell.... The bitches set me up man!" Richard recounted sadly. Loud laughter broke out as he described how his wife grabbed his gun and pointed it at him, demanding he kill the girl or she'd kill him.

"At first, I thought the bitch was joking until I looked in her eyes." He stared at his prison buddies. "The bitch was gonna kill me, sure as shit. She lost it, put the gun to the other two girls. Told me to grab some rope, give it to them and make them tie themselves up. I ain't lying. Then she pulls a knife from her purse and gives it to me.

"**WHAT THE FUCK IS THIS**?" I asked her. She looked over at the girl and told her to suck my dick. Now, I'm looking at this bitch like she's crazy, trying to see if this is the same woman I've been sleeping with for all these years."

By now Richard had an audience. And he told the story so remarkable that the prisoners resembled a group of small children being told a scary story.

"She made all three of them suck me off man!" Richard looks around the room. "You know what she had the fucking nerve to ask me afterwards. 'Do you love me?' Could you believe this bitch? Tears are rolling down her cheeks at this point."

"Of course I love you baby," I say trying to con her, but she wouldn't put that gun down. She was going to kill me and get this... She had the nerve to smile! Pointed the gun right at my head! Do you believe that shit?" Richard laughs out loud, still finding it hard to believe himself.

"So I say to her, honey, just tell me how I can make it up. Shit, in the past, a gift or jewelry always did the trick. There was always something that I could do to make her feel better when she caught me wrong." Richard shook his head. "Not this time." Staring out into the crowd of faces he'd been telling the same story to for over 10 years now, he continued.

"She wanted me to kill them." '*Either you kill these hoes right now or I will blow your goddamn head off starting with that little pecker you call a dick!*' The chick screams. I ain't gonna lie, I pissed in my pants."

"You can't be serious," I tell her. "But then the bitch gives me this look..." Richard connects with a fellow inmate. "All I can say is, that woman was not my wife. This bitch was possessed by the devil." Clyde locks eyes with his audience once again.

She looked into my eyes and said, "Don't make me do this."

She was going to kill my ass and I didn't wanna die. It was either them crack head bitches or me." He went on to describe how he stabbed the three women up, leaving them soaking in puddles of blood. Afterwards, he told how he set the women on fire, then left the scene. Richard stood there in a zone before the men. "Don't you know I stabbed the white whore over 10 times and the chick still ain't die. She ran outside, collapsed in the middle of the street.."

Black stares at the stranger, shaking his head as officers comes and ends their recreation time. "Ya'll white boys wild as shit.... Why didn't you just shoot the bitch?"

Richard considers the question and says, "Damn, I don't know! I've been in 10 years for this shit and never once thought about that."

Walking off, Black pats Richard on the shoulder and says, "You should've shot them hoes dawg. It's faster, plus you could've made sure they was dead."

Richard smiles amusingly at the young killer. "Yeah, well you got a

point there. I'll try and remember that in my next life time."

CHAPTER 24

It was the weekend and the hottest night spot in Petersburg was ju mping tonight, leaving the streets of Richmond deserted. The $500 reward for, 'shake yo ass,' contests always drew in an immense crowd. Grey Stone housing projects were bare with the exception of a few hungry flat footers, who decided to take advantage of the lack of competition.

Eco drove up about five or six cars, trailing behind in four clean Shark body Cadillac's. In the streets of Richmond, they were known as the Cadillac boys, riding through town one behind the other in a convoy. Downtown Petersburg was the livest spot in the city. Traffic was ridiculous. Party goers packed the streets.

Thug figures turned the Burger King parking lot into a car show. The marijuana was thick in the air. Many was trying to get their liquor and weed on before the club. Cops patrolled the streets as if a war was about to break out, intervening whenever they spotted a group of blacks hanging out. They hated Flavors night spot. Whenever the club was packed, it meant more work for them. Officers in the area knew there would be trouble. Fights that broke out inside the club always escalated to the parking lot. Many patrons feared those long stretches in the dark after the club. *It was a place where slugs rang out, leaving victims to rest: sometimes on their backs, but mostly face down on their chest.*

Rakee exits the passenger side of his LS 400 Lexus coupe and waits for his entourage as they park their flashy foreign whips in the clubs parking lot across the street. Players drove past slowly, scoping out the lovely ladies, waiting in line to get inside the nightclub. Tremendous ass and hips wobbled from the cuties in line every time the door opened and music would leak out. Rakee stood there fiddling with one of his 3' foot long braids, admiring a pretty red bone that walked past and winked at him. Relieved to finally see his boys heading over toward him, Rakee tipped the bouncer and his entire crew was allowed access to the club. Upon entering, he was immediately stunned by the prettiest face in the room.

"Oh my God!" Ayesha babbles out recklessly. "The nigga looking over here!"

"Damn, those niggas looking like money," adds Trina, pinching Tiffany's arm to get her attention"

"Shit girl, I think he's calling us," Ayesha raves in excitement. "I'm going to see what he wants."

These were the type of guys that every down chick wanted to be around. Before Tiffany could blink, she was inside the club, drinking champagne and partying in VIP. From where she sat in the VIP section, she spotted the photographer on the floor snapping photos and pondered over the idea of taking a cute picture for Jeffrey. But when taking in the revealing outfit she had on, she quickly decided against it. Plus she knew Jeffrey wouldn't approve of the skin tight bodysuit that highlighted every precious curve. Tiffany definitely had it going on and Rakee couldn't seem to keep his eyes off of her. Before leaving, Rakee told Tiffany to stop acting like a little girl and have a drink with him. He walked off before she could respond.

"Y'all are so nasty," Tiffany shouts out at both of her friends in the middle of the dance floor, backing up some amateur who couldn't handle a lot of ass at one time. Feeling out of place, Tiffany kept her place against the wall. 'Nearly five months since Jeffrey had been gone,' Tiffany was thinking as she noticed a group of girls, pointing and snickering in her direction.

Straining to recognize one of the familiar faces, Tiffany notices a girl she went to school with. Trina and Ayesha walked up, breathing heavily just in time to see Tiffany's expression. "Those stupid bitches keep staring at me..."

With breakneck speed, Tiffany and Ayesha looks over at the girls and shoots ice grills over in their direction. Trina turns to Tiffany.

"That's the bitch I was telling you about.... Keisha. The one in the middle. We went to school with her. I told you that Jeffrey was fucking her! Them bitches probably over there talking about it right now."

Tiffany's eyes beam with fire. The girl who Trina mentioned was gorgeous and secretly, Tiffany was intimidated. And she had every right to be. Keisha was hot! Had she been with Jeffrey?

"I'm gonna beat that bitches ass!" Tiffany attempted to storm over toward the girl clique but Trina grabbed her by the arm.
"Bitch, are serious? You got the freshest nigga in the club tonight trying to get at you. Them dumb bitches ain't nothing but a waste of time."

"Jeffrey ain't shit!" Ayesha blurts out. "Let's go back up to the VIP with Rakee and them. Come on girl, shit! Jeffrey is locked up anyway. And I'm trying to drink." Ayesha laughs. "Them niggas buying too."

"*Bitches ain't shit!*" Eco states at the disgusting sight of Tiffany and her friends crashing the party all hoochiefied. He took one look at the provocative way Tiffany was dressed and shook his head. Tiffany was killing the skin tight bodysuit. He downed his third glass of Remy Martin.

"You see, this is exactly the reason why I ain't got a girl!" As the liquor started to take an effect on Eco, he moved his hands in emphasis to his speech. "My nigga ain't been gone five months and already this bitch sitting in here up under some clown as nigga! You see what the bitch got on?" The fellas all agree that Tiffany is just a tad bit too much.

"Them hoes dick riding a nigga because he buying them drinks. I should go over there and cuss her ass out."

Tiffany tried her hardest not to scream. How long had Jeffrey's friends been watching her? 'There ain't no way I'm getting out of this one.' BUSTED! Her thoughts drifted back to Keisha and all of a sudden, sexual images of that tramp and Jeffrey together began to take over. "**He probably fucked the bitch!!**"

"Don't let me find out you talking to yourself." Rakee remarks jokingly but clearly sees that she is bothered by something. "What's good shorty? You don't seem to be enjoying yourself." He happen to then look over in the direction she was staring in and notice Eco and his boys eye balling their table from across the room. 'He probably did fuck that bitch!' Tiffany felt like a fool.

She manages a smile when refocusing back on Rakee standing next to her. "Yeah I'm okay."

"I see you got some admirers. What up with them?"

"Nothing, they're just friends of my boyfriend, Jeffrey."

"Okayyy... But the homey locked up right?"
"Yeah unfortunately."
Rakee's lips forms into a devious smile and immediately, he starts to mark his prey. "It don't have to be unfortunate. Let's make the most out of a bad situation."

Still, the images of that heffa and her boo together alone, sharing intimacy, was torturing and not far from her mind. It made her flesh crawl. The more she thought of the betrayal, the more she started to consider Rakee's proposition.

"I ain't trying to get you into trouble." While refilling Tiffany's glass, Rakee moved in on her, close enough that she could feel his warm breath. "If you not comfortable, I'll take you home. As much as I'd like you to stay, what's the point if you not enjoying yourself."

Tiffany didn't respond right off. She was staring at Keisha and the guys who approached her. She was irresistible. Jeffrey wouldn't turn down such a fine piece of ass. She was certain of it.

CHAPTER 25

Three weeks in transit was one mean experience for Jeffrey. When-ever he left a facility, the **U.S. Marshals** chained him up like some sort of dangerous animal. He sunk his head low at a cute brown skinned girl, who nearly jumped into oncoming traffic to avoid walking on the same sidewalk as the prisoners.

Jeffrey's life couldn't get any worse. Only two years to serve and they shipped him to Lexington Kentucky. Surrounded by nothing but mountains, Jeffrey hated every single minute of it. Whenever a person arrived at a prison, they had an opportunity to make one call informing family members of their whereabouts. Jeffrey didn't want to talk to anyone but his baby. His heart pounded with the phone pressed to his face. Dis-appointed when no one picked up, he dialed Prince's number and caught Wanda. She almost had a fit when he told her where he'd been shipped.

Back in the holding cell, Jeffrey's mind worked overtime, wonder-ing where Tiffany was and if or not she was with someone. Face rested in his hands, he thought, "Damn, a nigga ain't gone never get a visit. The whole six months, he dreamed about arriving at a prison and finally be-ing able to hold and kiss his girl. If he could see her once a month, that would be satisfactory. His sisters were always in his thoughts, but it seemed like Tiffany was all he could think about. He missed her pretty smile and couldn't wait to get another call. Her voice was a necessity right now.

Stepping foot on the prison compound was a relief. Weeks of sleep-ing in holding cells could wear a body down. His back ached terribly from the steel bed he'd rested on for the past month. Federal prison wasn't the way he imagined it, a place where they only housed Drug Lords and King-pins. The place resembled a college campus. In route to his housing unit, the officer met Jeffrey outside his office, handed him a bed role and directed him to his bunk. The parking lot was a room of 30 to 40 beds, occupied by real life Vikings.

"Cuz ,do you know where 72 upper at?" Jeffrey asked a Latino guy upon entering the room.

"Over there homes," He responded in broken English and pointed Jeffrey in the right direction. Most of the inmates were either at work or the recreation center. After finding his way with no problem, he glanced down at the shrubs on his feet and remembered that he had to catch the laundry before they closed.

He made up his bed and headed out on the compound. It was lunch time, so everyone was standing around conversing as if they were at home on the block. He instantly took notice of a long line which of course had to be the laundry exchange. Eager to get out of his bus clothes and into some fresh khakis, Jeffrey hurriedly took his spot at the end of the line. The youngster looked around at all the foreign faces, feeling a bit out of place. He didn't recognize a single face. "I can't believe they sent me here!"

"What you want!" Veteran laundry guy barks at Jeffrey."

"Just got here today, I guess I need everything."

"Got an ID?"

Jeffrey retrieves his ID card from his back pocket, hands it over to the tobacco chewing redneck officer. Jeffrey observes the man as he spat tobacco juice in the grass. After scribbling something down on paper, the officer gave back the ID card and instructed Jeffrey to return at 1 PM. That worked out fine. His stomach had begun to cramp, alerting him that it was time to eat.

A new comer always stood out in prison. Bus shoes and tight T-shirts were an instant giveaway, not to mention the young pants that stopped just below the ankles. Pausing in the middle of the floor as he stepped inside the dining hall, Jeffrey tried to figure out which line to get in. It amazed him to see brothers eating on one side and whites and Hispanics on the other side.

Naturally, Jeffrey falls in behind a Haitian brother with the longest dreadlocks he'd ever seen. After standing in line for what seemed an eternity, he sat down at an empty table across from a group of brothers who had a slightly distinguished look about them. Jeffrey dug into his meal while observing the men across from him. They wore their khaki suits pressed and their boots were spit shine cleaned.

Jeffrey finished his food and guzzled the last of the ice cold Pepsi. Looking around, he noticed a line of people holding empty trays. He fell in line, remembering he had to catch his counselor back at his office to get his PAC number. Each inmate were given a PAC number (ten digit number to activate their phones) to call home.

It had been almost a month since he talked to Tiffany. Plus he needed money for canteen, hygiene and everything else that made a bid more comfortable. It was 12:50 when he left the dining hall. The laundry line wasn't long as Jeffrey had predicted. After a five minute wait, he had his laundry bag and was on his way back to his housing unit.

The Ghost

CHAPTER 26

Tiffany had been feeling guilty ever since the night she went out. For weeks, she awaited Jeffrey's call. She knew that Eco would tell Jeffrey what he saw the first chance he got. Although she didn't see anything wrong with having a few drinks with friends, she knew he wouldn't approve of her chilling at a club around other guys. She took Rakee's number but never called him. A part of her wanted to hear his voice but then the other half said no and be there for her man as she'd promised. Despite the fact that he only had a two year sentence and her heart was desperately trying to remain faithful, yet her body yearned for a man's touch. Sometimes, she'd lie in bed and cry from loneliness. She missed his frequent hugs and kisses that she'd grown accustomed to.

Plenty of nights, Tiffany would sat and stare at Rakee's number and reach for the phone. In the same instant, she cursed Jeffrey for leaving her lonely. But then the guilt would kick in. His being there on her account was such a weighty burden. He never said anything to her personally, but she knew that deep down in Jeffrey's heart, he resented her for being locked up. So in spite of it all, she struggled to stay positive, even though it wouldn't be easy with a man like Rakee constantly invading her thoughts.

Tiffany's friends didn't help the situation at all, so she slowly began to distant herself from them. She needed to talk to her man and tell him about the feelings she'd been having, hoping Eco hadn't gotten to him first. Her mind was so far from schoolwork. She just sat there in six period in a daze. At 1:55, the bell sounded off as Tiffany grabbed her books and moved hastily toward the exit. Teenagers didn't waste time at the end of class. They moved swiftly down the long hallway as if a fire drill was in progress, making their way to the many buses lined up outside. Everybody loved George Wilkerson High School, especially after school. The parking lot resembled a block party.

Flashy whips, sound systems basing the entire parking lot. Others sat in their vehicles and smoked marijuana with the burner in their laps on a drug free school zone, **talk about young and restless**. Shuffling through the pack of bodies, Tiffany acknowledges a few of her class mates and waves, but never stops on her way to her car. Surprisingly, as she was about to drive away, a Lexus coupe drives up and blocks her in. Before she could even react, the driver is out of his car calling her name. Tiffany hold the door, waiting for him to approach, trying hard not to stare at Rakee's solid frame outlined in a wife beater.

His Rolex glistens in the sunlight. "What up Tiff? I see you ain't use that number I gave you."

"Look Ra-"

"I Apologize for cutting you off. But let me say this... I like you... A lot. I ain't a nigga just out to get some ass."

"What else could you possibly want then?"

"Come on Tiff, pussy come a dime a dozen, but on some real nigga shit, I fucks with you. But I see you trying to keep shit tight with yo nigga..." Rakee cracks a wide grin. "You need to come and play for a winning team though."

His attractive brown eyes causes her to breathe heavily. Blushing terribly, Tiffany expresses deep gratitude, even going so far as thanking him, but made sure that he understood where her loyalty was.

"Shorty, if I can't be nothing else, let a nigga be yo friend. I don't want nothing from you. If you need anything just holla, aight?"

At a loss for words, Tiffany simply nods her head in acknowledgment.

"Oh, I got something for you." Rakee disappears into the Lexus, lifting a box from the passenger seat. Tiffany observes him with suspicion, wondering what was in the huge crate, chuckling as she waited in suspense.

"Here you go. I hope you like it. Go ahead and open it."

Lifting the top slowly, her eyes flashes with excitement. "It's so pretty, Rakee!!" Tiffany gently raise the beautiful bluish gray pit bull puppy from the box, bringing it to her chest to hug it.

Rakee marvels at Tiffany's bright face. It was nice to see her smiling for a change. "You like it?"

"I love it!!" Tiffany replied as she kissed the puppy. While she was busy admiring her new found friend, Rakee loaded a couple month's supply of Eukanuba dog food and various toys into her backseat. When he was done, he let his hand glide through the puppy's smooth coat of fur while never taking his eyes away from Tiffany.

"Jeffrey's one lucky nigga."

They were now gazing into one another's eyes and Tiffany could feel her body responding in more ways than one. Rakee leans over and steals a kiss.

"I'm glad you like your puppy," he says before smoothly walking off. He just left her there! She watches Rakee's car make a left turn, disappearing on to Midlothian tnpk. Placing her gift back in the crate, Tiffany throws the car in gear and drive away with a lot to ponder over.

The Ghost

CHAPTER 27

Prince was in deep contemplation after leaving Prince George County. The news about Jeffrey being shipped so far away from home had him feeling uneasy. He called the boy's attorney, Jennings to ask why they had transferred him so far, but his only reply was, **the Feds operate that way**. Prince was all too familiar with prison life, so he quickly purchased several money orders, totaling over 2,500 and sends them first class.

He didn't want Jeffrey to have to wait or want for anything. The boy had been through enough already and it was time for things to start turning around. The O G just hoped that Jeffrey would come home a better man. The worst thing a convict could do, was leave prison the same way they went in. Things were going well. Erica and Britney were ecstatic about the fact that they'd soon be in their new home. Only three more months to go for the custody hearing, Prince had been having such a good time with the girls and the three had developed a tight relationship. He admired Erica's intelligence as well as how remarkably strong she'd remained through all of this.

They spent weekends together, visiting somewhere different each time. He got a kick out of just seeing them happy. He was set on giving back, confident that God would be pleased and possibly eradicate some of his bad Karma.

Prince cut out the lights after parking inside his garage. Glancing up at the window, he spotted Wanda in the kitchen, putting together one of her delicious dishes. As soon as he opened the door, the boy charged at his father and Prince swooped him up and into his arms.

"Dad, where you been?"

"You know yo daddy a workaholic." Father and son sat down on the sofa.

"Mama is cooking chicken tonight," the boy states cheerfully. Wanda appears in the doorway with a delighted smile on her face.

"Daddy, come and play the game with me. You promised yesterday, remember?"

"I did, didn't I. Well, a promise is a promise, go and set the game up." Wanda took a seat next to her man and greeted him gently with a kiss.

"Erica has been calling and asking when are we going to see Jeffrey." Prince releases a deep sigh and she detects that something is bothering him. "What is it baby?"

"Nothing... I won't be able to go and see Jeffrey.... Make sure that Erica and Britney makes it down to see him though, okay."
Evidently, he had a good reason why he couldn't go and see Jeffrey, so she didn't question why. "Okay baby, I got it."

"Thanks boo," he gave her a passionate kiss on her lips. "I appreciate that." Then the couple laughed at the sound of Pernell calling out for his father to come and play the game. "Let me go and play with him before he wake up the whole damn neighborhood." Prince kissed his woman then he disappeared into the room with Pernell.

CHAPTER 28

F.C.I Lexington housed 2500 inmates, the majority of which were Blacks and Hispanics. The compound could easily be mistaken for a college campus the way the dormitories were set up. Prisoners had to work and attend class and GED was a requirement. Age was not a factor in the Feds. 80 year old men would stroll to school right along with the youngsters.

Jobs paid next to nothing. Two cents an hour wasn't enough to feed a small child. Nevertheless, inmates worked long hours, especially the institutionalized brothers who'd been bidding for a long time. Prison was a world within a world. Those coming straight off the streets were mind blown. Men sexing men was a way of life behind the walls. Some cats walked around with their guy like they were a couple, and would fight or cut another prisoner attempting to come on to their queer. In prison, the homosexuals were the women and knives were guns. They lived like beauty queens in the prison system. On the compound, there was this one cat whom his clients named, "The Guzzler." It was said that he earned such a name because he sucked off a dozen penises a day."

Gangs ran the compound, controlling everything profitable: from drugs, gambling, even prostitution. Some guys pimped homosexuals, making them bring back whatever money they made from turning tricks. The Gangster Disciples were the oldest and largest black gang around. They were deep in Lexington, constantly in conflict with the Vice Lords, another notorious group.

Bloods and Crips were in the prison as well but the numbers were small. Islam Nation was the second largest black group on the compound.

All of the black organizations kept their eyes open for new recruits, especially youngsters coming into the system for the first time. There were a lot of game spitters in the Feds, just like the streets, because the same cat's in prison were once in free society. A person had to really be careful when meeting a stranger. Many had agendas and there could be a number of reasons. Brothers would often find that guys who started off as cool, were actually undercover fags, befriending them for no other reason than to attempt to turn them out.

Jeffrey could peep game when it came to making friends. After going to the store and spending his entire limit, he was able to relax a little. Adjusting wasn't so hard after getting everything that he needed. He called everyone to let them know his location. He finally reached Tiffany and had been on the phone with her most of the day. Her voice relaxed him and he didn't even speak much of the incident at the club. He was just happy that she was there. However, Tiffany did catch him off guard when she inquired about his sexual relations with Keisha. But being the straight forward guy that he was, Jeffrey of course the denied allegations.

He couldn't wait to curse out Keisha for the little show she and her friends put on at the club for Tiffany. His second day there, Jeffrey found out that there were only ten or twelve guys from Richmond Virginia on the compound. Scooter was a Petersburg native and knew Jeffrey was from VA the first time he laid eyes on him. After giving the youngster a rundown on the institution and its rules, Scooter showed him where everything was located. He explained how VA was outnumbered and how everyone on the East Coast stuck together. Scooter had already served six years on a 15 year bid. He pretty much knew everybody and warned Jeffrey about how the gangs tried to cut into youngsters like himself.

They sat inside the TV room passing a Black and Mild back and forth, watching videos. Jeffery's head was spinning from inhaling the strong smoke from the cigar. It had been months since he'd smoked anything.

His mind started to drift away to the streets, unable to rid his thoughts of Tiffany. He'd had enough of the phone for one day, especially after talking to Eco. Moping around, trying to picture his girl sitting at a table under some dude drinking, was starting to eat away at Jeffery. He wondered if she would've told him about that night had Eco not been there.

Jeffery took a long drag off the Black, passed it to Scooter, then stepped off. He waited impatiently for a Jamaican cat to finish his conversation. Though Tiffany told him he had nothing to worry about, he needed reassurance, so the minute the phone was available, Jeffery hurriedly went over and got on it. He waited for the loud intercom to announce the ten minute move before dialing.

When Scooter saw Jeffrey on the phone, he shook his head, knowing instantly what he was doing. Fresh in the system, Scooter reacted in the same way in trying to keep tabs on his girl from prison.

"Yo Jeff! Can't do it like that, mane. Come on cuz, let's go outside and get us some air. **No one answered**. He did his best to conceal his disappointment upon hanging up the phone. He jetted off to grab his radio and met Scooter by the exit where they headed out to the yard.

Stepping across the compound, Jeffery asked his new friend about the sharp brothers standing in front of the chapel. "That's the Islam Nation. Yeah they fishing, trying to get motherfuckers to come watch tapes and shit."

"Peace soldiers," Brother Akim says. "We got a beautiful tape we showing tonight. Come in and get you some knowledge."

"Naw, not today bro mane, maybe next week," Scooter replied. Jeffery felt the man eying him. "What about you, beloved? You new on the pound?"

"Yeah... I'm Jeffrey."

"Where you from?"

"Richmond VA," Jeffery replied bluntly.

Akim smiled and never took his eye away from Jeffrey. "You brothers look like you in a hurry. I'll see you next week, right?" The two glanced at each other before saying yes, as they exchanged handshakes before parting ways. On the yard, guys were everywhere. The summer league basketball game was going on. Crowds of inmates surrounded the blacktop, watching Trick Dave put on a show. He was said to be the best player in the BOP. He could do anything with a ball and whenever his team played, nobody wanted to miss it. Trick Dave was from Virginia Beach. On the streets, he was a legend and over the ten years he'd been doing time, he still received much love from the streets. Every month he had a different hottie traveling down to see him, some even flying in from different parts of the country.

In the late 80's, Dave and his brother were busted with over 30 kilos of pure powder. The Feds wanted the whole family, but the two stuck to their guns and went hard and held their water. The brothers were well known, even in the system. Trick Dave was still making lots of money from gambling tickets he ran. His money was long, and nobody could fade him.

Cats loved this guy, gangs even. They showed mad love. One would never suspect that he had a 30 year sentence. It was funny how people on the streets thought that everybody was miserable in prison. Of course, there were some in that state, but there were also the soldiers, who accepted their sentences and made the best out of their situation.

Trick Dave came down the court, crossing one cat up, almost breaking his ankles, then hit his fifth three- pointer, sending the crowd into a frenzy!!! Jeffery thought he was watching Jordan or somebody.

"The nigga like that!" He yelled excitedly.

Queers were even sitting in their own corner, hollering out his name like cheerleaders. "Go Dave!!" A short, ape looking homo belts out.

Scooter laughs, watching Jeffery stare at the group of men lovers in astonishment. "Come on, lets walk the track." Making their way onto the big field's track, Scooter spotted five of the homies from different parts of VA. They joined the fellows in a lap around the track. Everyone spoke, giving each other dap as they met up. Out of the four, there was one cat named Scooter, that Jeffrey admired the most. He and Joe had been bidding together for four years. Born and raised in Petersburg, Joe was 24 years old with 12 more years to serve. His father was a thoroughbred name Eli, who made a fortune kiting checks and milking banks dry. Eli gave his son everything he wanted, including a Benz for his 18th birthday. All Joe had to do was stay out of the streets.

Of course, he went behind his father's back and brought some weight in cocaine. Months passed and he started to do well for himself. The Feds were already on to his pops, but couldn't nab him because his game was that tight. An informant went to agents saying Joe was hustling. They figured if they couldn't get Eli, they'd get the next best thing.

The DEA caught him red handed with a kilo of crack and told him all he had to do was set his father up. Joe told the Feds to eat a dick, went to trial and lost. So there he was, in Federal Prison, being the soldier he was raised to be. Eli turned totally legit and took care of his son well, sending five hundred a month. He visited at least twice a month, and supported his son to the fullest. The time hadn't really gotten to Joe yet, maybe because he stayed high all of the time, running and trying not to think about the next twelve years.

Scooter and the gang found a nice spot where nobody was, possible only because all the inmates on the field were watching a softball game. A tower was in the sky, but the operator was about 60 years old and all she did was smoke cigarettes and sleep. The compound truck, circled outside the institution's perimeter fence whenever it felt like it and could easily be seen coming from a safe distance away. Scooter relaxed back on the bench, while Jeffrey sat by his side. Just looking at the weed smoke got Jeffrey high. He pulled hard, started coughing and passed the blunt to Joe. "Goddamn!"

"Nigga, I told you it was some fire." Laughter broke out.

"You alright?" Asked Scooter. "I swear Jeffery, I'd hate to have to leave yo ass out here."

"I'm good.... I'm good.................. Let me hit that shit again."

"That's what I'm talking about," Ray Bob says, passing the weed.

"Spark this shit then, since we smoking," Joe says, pulling another torpedo out of his khaki shirt pocket. Jeffery's eyes were beyond bloodshot. He hadn't smoked in so long that the weed took an instant effect. The youngster looked up at his new buddies.

"Y'all niggas dun peeled my shit back to the white meat! **I AM HIGH!**" Everybody roars with laughter as they continue to pass the blunts back and forth.

By now, they were cracking jokes on each other and laughing uncontrollably. Ray Bob even went so far as to imitate a one handed swing being executed by a severely handicap player in the softball game. After his sick performance, all of the members of the group struggled to catch their breaths. One guy laughed so hard that slob leaked out of his mouth.

Joe turned to his partner and slurred. "Ain't no way I'm walking across the compound like this!"

"Yeah, we gotta stay down here until recall," replied Scooter.

Jeffery stands up, almost falling as he staggers, then quickly sat back down.

"Damn yo, I can't move right now!"

CHAPTER 29

Jeffrey was an excellent poet. His words were deep and touched the innermost, essential part of a person's heart. He tried desperately to hold on to Tiffany by writing love poems every week, encouraging her to be strong and protect the sacredness of their relationship. He assured her that things would be better than before. Every month like clockwork, she'd come down to visit and would rent a hotel room for the weekend just to be near her boo. Jeffrey loved it and looked forward to seeing her. He had become dependent on her for mental and moral support. Tiffany was all he could think of day and night. And she tried her best to show Jeffrey the love he needed. It didn't matter what she was doing when it came to her boo, she'd stop everything and make herself available. But as the months passed, Tiffany began to feel exhausted from the phone calls, visits, and worst of all, having to go home to an empty bed.

"Why should I have to stop my life?" The question became a constant nagging pain in her a$$!!! Though he only had a year left to do, she craved for loving right now!! Not a year from now!!! Tiffany needed someone to hold her down today. She was sick of concealing her feelings and looking Jeffrey in the eyes and lying. Living two lives wasn't easy and was beginning to be downright complicated. How could she tell Jeffrey that she'd manage to fall in love with another man? Rakee had swept her off her feet and she couldn't even recall how it happened...

Tiffany was caught up. The more time she spent with Rakee, the deeper her feelings grew. He understood the relationship she had with Jeffrey and out of respect, he never interfered. When Jeffrey would call her, he'd make sure she accepted the call, although at times she didn't want to, especially when they just finished banging it out. There was no question that she still loved Jeffrey, Rakee simply came around at the right time. It was easier to love someone who was present. The letters and poems weren't enough. Jeffrey wasn't there and that was the advantage Rakee had over him, not to mention the flashy materialistic life style that he lived.

Rakee was a playa and sadly, Tiffany was just another stallion in his stable. He put his game down and got her just the way he planned. He knew that something as small as a puppy meant a lot to a girl like Tiffany. It was a solid invesment. She simply needed someone to replace that frown with a smile. And it didn't take much. He wined and dined her, took her shopping and they flew out to Vegas for a weekend and had a blast.

Tiffany constantly compared the two men in her life, 'Jeffrey ain't never did this for me. He never bought this or took me there...' Confused about the whole situation, she went to her mother for advice. She loved Jeffrey but she was in love with Rakee. "Mama what should I do?"

"Baby, you say you falling in love with this boy... But how does he feel about you? See honey, it's easy for us women to fall in love. It don't take much," Mama smiles. "We can feel a nice piece of meat and go crazy. And you know how we love money." Mother and daughter shared a laugh as she went on. "All we really want is love. We might already have it and not even realize it. **Sometimes, it's just better to love the person who loves you, instead of the one you claim to love. True love is hard to find darling**."

CHAPTER 30

Chesterfield Town Center was located on the outskirts of Richmond. Not too many city folks traveled to the mall because of the distance, but every now and then, city goers would visit the mall. It was 7 o'clock when Eco drove up and parked outside the mall's parking lot. Eco had one of the prettiest Cadillac's in the city, but it had nothing on the shiny Lexus parked in front of him. Looking at it only made him want to put in over time on the block to get one for himself. His partners, Marlo and Kareem marveled at the car as well.

It was Friday and the three were at the mall to find some fresh gear to wear out tonight. While waiting for a vehicle to pass so that they could go inside the mall, Eco's chaw drops to the ground. "I can't believe this shit!"
Soon afterward, his buddies shared similar expressions as they stood in utter silence, watching Tiffany and her new love leave the mall with shopping bags. And to top it off, the couple walked to the same overly priced Lexus he'd been drooling over only minutes ago. "*Look at this sneaky bitch!*" Eco states in fury.

"Damn, shorty girl is foul," adds Kareem. The three friends shake their heads. "I want that bitch to know I see her ass! You got that burner on you, right. Just in case this nigga pop some slick shit." Kareem gestures to the bulge in his jacket to confirm that he did in fact have his weapon on him.

Tiffany lowers her head in shame at the sight of Eco and a couple of Jeffrey's friends. She cursed herself for not recognizing the Cadillac parked in front of Rakee's Lexus. Locking eyes, she spoke to the three familiar faces as they approached the car.

Marlo watched Rakee like a hawk. "What's this shit cuz?" Rakee inquired, eying each man with suspicion.

"Playa this ain't got nothing to do with you," Marlo quickly fore-warns Rakee. Immediately upon observing the pistol on Marlo's hip, Rakee didn't try and put up a fight. Tiffany looked at Rakee for confirmation before pulling Eco to the side.

"You gonna tell Jeffrey, ain't you?"

"What the fuck type question is that? Damn Shorty, why you doing my nigga like this? I mean cuz be home in less than a year."

"Eco, if you tell him, all its going to do is stress him out. Please, he don't need to know this right now."
Eco caught himself, he almost called her out of her name.

"What the hell type friend would I be if I sit here and allow you to play my man like that. He needs to know you ain't shit, straight like that."

"But Eco,"

"Naw, fuck that! Ain't no sense in you keep leading him on. Want me to tell him or you do it? You can't have your cake and eat it too." Eco walks off before she could muster a response, leaving her looking like a lost child. Tears streams down her cheeks as she flutters over to Rakee's waiting arms. After a couple minutes of comforting her, they get inside the car and drive away.

CHAPTER 31

Some of the smartest men in the world were wasting away behind prison walls. Moves were still being made inside the system. Cats were running numbers, dope peddling, playing poker and doing just about anything to make a dollar. Some guys took care of their families from prison. Most of the business was conducted on the yard. Under the hut beside the softball field, there sat six tables occupied by the top poker players in the prison. If a person wasn't in the game, then they had to keep stepping. Standing around the table only made the spot hot. Trick Dave's partner O'shay, ran the poker table and didn't allow any bystanders.

Jeffrey stayed away from the tables. After leaving Scooter on the softball field, he decided to walk some laps. The weed he'd just smoked had him stoned, only making him more depressed than he was before. Thoughts of Tiffany were fresh in his mind. He made his way over to the basketball court and posted up where a full court basketball game was in session.

Two cats were fussing. The taller dude from Baltimore dunked on his shorter homeboy, hollering, "*my nuts in yo mouth,*" as he hung from the rim. Jeffrey notice how blacks were the most separated out of all the races. Various religion sectors were out on the yard in their individual corners.

After visiting the chapel and hearing brother Akim speak, he gained a deeper understanding for the Islam Nation. Scooter even took him to one of the, Nation of Gods and Earths ciphers. Listening to the two groups, there was still something bothering Jeffrey. If both groups believed that the black man was the original man, then why were they building separately, instead of together?

Jeffrey was high, but focus. It saddened him to see how divided his people were. Reflecting back on some of the conversations he'd have with his mother, he remembered talking about this same thing he was now witnessing with his own two eyes. Christians were standing outside of the gym, while the Gods formed a circle around the empty basketball court. Rasta's were deep as well, sitting directly across from the Islam Nation. All of these groups were searching to find God, whether it be in the sky or on the ground, not realizing that each and every one of them would remain lost until they found one another. **Until one found self... God would forever be a mystery**.

Jeffrey felt sick inside, trying his hardest not to think the worst. Tiffany hadn't written in three weeks. Every time he called, the phone just rang. He knew something was wrong when she didn't show up this last past weekend. The youngster made up all types of excuses for why she hadn't written or answered the phone. And he didn't want to jump to any conclusions about the information Eco had given him. He simply refused to believe that she was out there in a relationship.

Mail Call had become a stressful period of the day. He would stand there hopelessly, praying to himself as the officer called out names. No one had heard anything from Tiffany. He'd even gotten Erica to call her, but Tiffany never answered. When the ten minute move was announced, Jeffrey hurried up to the gate after hours of strenuous work out and waited for the recreation officer to open it. Back in the housing unit, he rushed straight to the phone.

Jeffrey slammed the phone down, cursing violently! The C O walked out of his office and into the hallway, sniffing around for the source of the commotion. All he could see was the rear of an angry prisoner storming to the parking lot bed area.

"Aye homey, did you get the letter I put under your pillow?" A tall, slim inmate from Portsmouth Virginia named Mike asked. Looking up at the figure, Jeffrey finally realized the guy was talking to him.

"Damn cuz, you alright?" Mike asked, noticing the blank expression on Jeffrey's face. Answering with a quick nod of the head, it was clear that Jeffrey wasn't in the mood for any conversing. Mike gave him a friendly pat on the shoulder, reminding him about the letter, then walked off.

After getting the letter, he sat back down and stared at the envelope. At the mere sight of Tiffany's name, Jeffrey get a burst of relief.

"This bitch better have a damn good excuse for not getting at me," he mumbles while quickly opening the envelope.

Dear Jeffrey,

How are you doing? Everything is alright on this end. I know you've been cursing me out. By now, I'm sure you talk to Eco. Baby, I'm sorry I let you down. I haven't been in contact with you and that's only because I didn't know what to say. Yes, I'm seeing someone else and somehow my feelings are deeply involved.
I thought I could do this two years with you, but it's not as easy as you think. I'm lonely out here and right now the man I'm with is giving me everything I need. Sorry I had to say this to you in a letter, but to be honest, I can't even look you in the eyes right now. I still love you, that will never change. I just can't do this no more. Don't think this isn't hard for me because I feel like shit leaving my man while he's down. I don't even know what I'm doing, all I know is I hate being alone.
I gave your clothes and money to Wanda. Hope you didn't mind me using a few hundred for bills. Please don't hate me. I hope we can still be friends. I think it may be best if you not call anymore. That will make it a lot easier for both of us. Well again, I apologize for going about it this way. You are a soldier so I know you will get over this. Life goes on, take care of yourself okay... Bye

Love, Tiffany

Jeffrey's eyes are rain tears as he reads the letter over and over, totally dumbfounded by the contents of what he was reading. He stood up and hastily made his way to the nearest phone, nearly running over a tiny Asian guy. Those who knew Jeffrey simply stood back and observed him angrily punch in numbers repeatedly to no avail. The scene had been played out many times before behind the prison walls. *Women breaking out on their men once they got locked up.* Jeffrey was hurting inside and didn't care who knew.

"How could this be happening to me?!" He pleaded with God to not let this be his reality. He felt like he was about to die inside. After dialing Tiffany's number several times, Jeffrey called his boy Eco to confide in him.

"**Let her go my nigga,**" was Eco's response. Jeffrey slammed the phone down in his ear, unable to deal with Eco right now. He was in love with this girl and he wasn't about to let her slip away without a fight. He wouldn't be able to rest if he didn't respond back to her immediately.

"I ain't hearing this shit!!!" Jeffrey grabs a pen and notepad from his locker. "This bitch can't do this to me!"
At the table, he stares at the blank paper and began to write.

Tiffany,

Shorty, what the fuck is the deal with you??!! How you gone write me some bullshit like this? You ain't wrote me nor have you brought your ass down here to see me, now you won't even answer your telephone. What have I ever done to deserve this? I'm sitting in this bitch, suffering for some shit you did! And you have the nerve to write me some bullshit like this. How you let this happen?
You been lying to me all this time. I thought you loved me. What happened to that? Just a year I been gone and you ready to cut out already??? You let a nigga come and take you away like that? Did you even fight? And you say you love me, where is the love? Leave a nigga when he down and out!! You know I need you. Please babe, you can't do this shit to me now!!
Answer the phone so that we can talk. Don't do me like this, shorty. You got a nigga in here fucked up. I love you Tiff, don't let

nobody take you away from me like that. This is too much for me to handle right now. I never thought I'd see the day when you'd treat me so foul. I'm sitting here looking at this letter and I just can't believe it's from you. Shorty, think about what you doing. Is the dick that good? He doesn't love you like I do. A year left Tiffany, ain't I worth it?

I won't accept this!! We suppose to be better than this. Do you realize what you putting me through?! I hope and pray that we can get past this because I can't do a bid like this. I love you... Come back home..

Jeffrey

The Ghost

CHAPTER 32

The ride from seeing Jeffrey was long and quiet. Brittany slept the whole trip, while Wanda and Erica discussed her brother's situation. Both could easily tell that problems between Jeffrey and Tiffany had flared and was affecting him tremendously, especially at the mention of Tiffany. Erica wanted to throw blows at the girl for doing her brother that way.

It was supposed to have been a good visit. Only one more week and they'd be in court. The girls were so excited and wanted their brother to share the same joy. But the only thing that seemed to make him smile was Brittany. She demanded to have her brother's attention. Erica left disappointed, wishing there was something more she could do for Jeffrey. At one time during their visit, she could have sworn that he was on the brink of tears.

Brittany was still asleep when they pulled in front a spacious three story home in North Richmond. Prince was already at the door waiting. Erica moved to the backseat as the O G made his way toward the vehicle. Prince could sense something wrong the minute he got in and observed their expressions. He immediately turned to Wanda for answers.

"So how was the visit?" Both Wanda and Erica were hesitant to speak. He spun around in his seat and says to Erica, "Is he okay?"

"He doesn't looks good to me," replied Erica as the car drives off.

"Okay, so he messed up about that girl right?"

"Yeah and in a bad way too," Erica says and shakes her head, struggling to hold back tears.

Unbeknown to anyone inside the car, Prince cut an eye over at Wanda and cracked a sly smile. "Yeah, I know exactly what he going through."

She immediately looks over at him and says, "Oh, so you do?"
Smoothly rubbing his goatee, Prince nods his head. "Hell yeah I know a lil bit about that. Your girl leave you while you locked down, it ain't a good feeling.... But Jeffrey a warrior, he'll bounce back Fasho."

Wanda remained silent. She hated to be reminded of that dark period in their lives. Although he had forgiven her, every now and then he would pop shots at her like now. It was a personal joke between the couple. Prince was very much aware that he hit a nerve, however; Jeffrey and Tiffany's ordeal did hit home.

"I didn't know he cared for Tiffany like that," admitted Erica. Prince was still watching his wife to be out of the corner of his eye, very much aware that she'd been affected by his comment. He leaned over to kiss her softly on her brown cheek, reassuring her of his love. He kissed her hand and looked back at the girls. Brittany was wide awake when they parked in front of the foster care building. "Are y'all ready to move into your house?"

"Yesssss!" Britney bounces up and down ecstatic.

Erica simply smiles at her sister, relieved that the nightmare was finally coming to an end. She was so ready to leave this place but didn't want to show her excitement. So much had happened to her family within the last few months that it seemed like no relief would ever come for them. If something didn't happen for them soon, she felt like she was gonna need a shrink.

"Hey y'all, cheer up... One more week," Prince assures them as they exit the SUV and walk up to the front entrance. Mrs. Anderson is there to meet them at the door with a huge smile.

"How was your weekend?" Brittany rambled on and on to the case-worker about their interesting weekend. Erica and Wanda embraced for a hug while Brittany leaped into Prince's arms.

He kissed her fluffy cheeks then hugged Erica. "We gone call you tonight, okay." The girls disappeared into the building, leaving the adults alone to talk.

"Next week," the caseworker reminded the couple. "Are you two ready?"

"We can't wait," both answered simultaneously.

"Our son loves them." Wanda adds.

"Don't worry, Judge Roberts will grant custody." Anderson winks her eye." Bright and early now."

The girls stood there in the doorway as the couple waved goodbye and drove away.

The Ghost

CHAPTER 33

It only took 10 minutes to get across town. Wanda made a left turn onto the bridge, driving slowly pass Mosby Middle which was renamed after the late great, Martin Luther King. Prince stared at the housing projects across the street, reflecting back on the old days when his crew was on the streets. Before the gun play and vicious street wars, they used to fight it out regularly with cats from these projects. He attended Mosby Middle for a couple of years and often wished that he could rewind back the hands of time when life wasn't so serious. Much had changed in recent years.

He'd sit at times, reminiscing about his boys and wondering how they were holding up in prison. Often times, he felt guilty being the only and last member of the notorious gang, THE JUICE CREW still standing. He and Wanda discussed everything and when he'd start talking about not deserving happiness, she would quickly put him in check. One of his joys were the several Boys and Girls clubs he'd been an adamant supporter of for years. And just recently, four of them he furnished and as a extra treat for the kids, he put computers and pool tables inside them.

Children loved Prince and showed him much love whenever he visited any of the clubs. He'd even stay there and shoot a couple of games of pool with the trash talking teenagers. The Community Center on Commendation street in Mosby was one of his favorites, mainly because he built the structure from the ground up. Prince brought the burgundy house a year after his release. It was a shack when he first got it, but after spending a small fortune to tear down and rebuild, it easily became the best looking house on the block.

School was still in session when Wanda drove up to the property. Prince was impressed with how well kept the place looked, grass cut and bushes neatly trimmed. The couple watched as Prince's cousins towering frame stood, grinning on the side walk. Randy was brown skinned with a low cut Caesar. Fresh out of college, the 6'3 athlete was a star shooting guard for the VCU RAMS. His second year on the team, they made it to the Championship. On a fast break to score his 35th point, Randy was undercut in mid air by one of the rival players. He went down hard, shattering his ankle in three places and destroying his career.

Prince told Randy he would help him in any way that he could. The basketball star enjoyed working with kids, so Prince put him in charge of the youth center. He initially planned on renting the property out, but decided to put it to better use when Randy came along. After he obtained the child cares license, the rest was history. Prince got out of the truck and made his way over to his cousin.

"What's up cuz?" Randy was so happy to see Prince that he nearly lifted him off of his feet with a huge hug. "Why Wanda ain't come and holla at me?"

"I won't be along... Just wanted to stop through and check on you." Randy waves at Wanda sitting in the truck looking like a little girl. Prince turned to look at the shiny Mercedes parked in the driveway.

"Damn playa, you got that motherfucker blinging!"

"Yeah mane, I told you I would take care of it. Shit, it's the least I could do, you bought it for me."

"You earned it big cuz." Prince took a minute to examine the yard. "Everything looks good out here. So... All is well with the kids right..."

"Yeah they good. I told them the only way they could hang out here is if their good grades stay up. I got them working man. The girls love the computers too."

"Alright then, that's good." Prince replies. "What about the boys?"

"Some of them knuckle heads be on them but mostly, it just be the girls. They be roughing shit off."

"They laughed, discussing the children's progress and plans of securing a larger building. Prince admired his cousins ambition. As long as it was for the kids, Randy was on board. Prince knew that he overpaid him but his main concern was keeping Randy from off the streets. "So look cuz, if you need anything just hit me up."

"Alright Prince, you got to come see me more often."

Prince assured his cousin that he would, another embrace and they parted ways.

"You a good nigga Prince. I appreciate all this mane. I don't know where I'd be if it won't for you." His words drew in the biggest smile from Prince's face.

"We family, it's nothing." The phone rings from inside the house as Randy waves once more and then rushes inside to catch his call. Meanwhile, Prince turns on his heels and continues his stride toward the spacey SUV when suddenly someone calls his name. Prince instantly stops and turns to see a tall, lanky figure, jogging toward him from out of the projects, adjacent to their Center.

"What's good my G, I know you?" Prince observed him with suspicion as he approached and quickly extended his hand out.

"Probably not, it's been a minute Prince." The 6'2 stranger sported dark blue baggy jeans and dirty, black Air Max sneakers with a black hoodie covering his dreads.

"Its Ricky mane!" The guy was excited as if he was standing before a legend. The man's smile put Prince at ease.

"I got a terrible memory, where I know you from though, because you do look familiar?"

"You don't know me, but I know you. I lost my brother at one of your spots a while back. *The Club house.* The keyword for Prince was, (club house).

A loud voice boomed in Prince's head, sending shivers down his spine. He never took his eye off the man's eye's, frantically searching them for intent. Within the blink of an eye, the friendly smile turns sinister. Then he says it.

"You slumped my brother, do you rem-"

Prince didn't waste another second. He put it all together at the same time. With no other choice but to act hastily, the guy didn't finish his statement before Prince's fist went crashing into his face. The blows were quick and precise and he succeeded in stunning his attacker only momentarily. He stumbled backwards but quickly regained his ground. Anticipating his next move, Prince catches the reach! Then out comes the pistol!! Prince brakes into a sprint!!!

"Waaaaannda!" He screams it!!!! It was a desperate cry for help!!

Before she could react to her man's call, shots rang out!! She spots Prince battered and trying to zig zag hot shells as the guy attempts to silence him forever. No time to think, Wanda did the only sensible thing she could think of. *It was a natural reaction.* She was up out of the truck in no time, discharging a 380 pistol she kept hidden in her Louis Vuitton bag. The guy hadn't anticipated Wanda. The first shot exploded into his chest before he took notice of her. She fired her weapon at the assailant as he unsuccessfully tried to flee from the connecting slugs, only to collapse in the middle of the street.

Randy was the first to reach Prince. He heard the shots and dashed from the back of the house as soon as the shots first commenced. Prince was stretched out in Randy's arms when Wanda ran up to aid him.

"Just hold on cuz!!!" Shouted Randy. Wanda screamed hysterically as she observed the blood rapidly leaking from her man's body.

"Somebody call the ambulance god damn it!!! What the fuck are y'all looking at???!!!" Wanda snaps at the small group of people forming around them. She refocused her attention back down at Prince.

"Oh God Prince, stay with me baby." She pushed Randy to the side and tried to comfort the love of her life, wiping and kissing his face.

"Talk baby... Please talk to me!!"

Prince was delirious. As sirens sounded in the near distance, his breaths became shallow. The O G's eyes left Wanda's and rolled up to a cloudless sky as all movements ceased. A feeling of calmness and serenity suddenly surrounding him.

For every cause, there was an equal or even worse effect. There was no time statue on revenge. What went around, came back around, the law in which governed the entire universe. Years ago when Prince's crew was on the streets, Justice killed a guy. When his folks came back to kill Justice, Prince in return, killed him, leaving behind a mother to mourn two dead sons. He had forgotten all about the brother who had escaped. Almost 8 years later, Prince had virtually dismissed the life he'd taken from memory. He had protected his man, gone to prison and came home to make a comfortable life for himself.

Senseless murder is wrong, no matter the motive, especially genocide. Life is a roller coaster and people reap what they sow, so one should always be careful about their actions. A person could win for years, but eventually... Prince got caught slipping, another good brother gunned down in the streets. ***Charge it to the game.***

The Ghost

CHAPTER 34

Mr. Cooper was one of the few African American counselors at F.C.I Lexington. Unlike most of his coworkers, he actually gave a damn. He showed tremendous compassion for the brothers confined and often times went out of his way to help them. Most counselors and officers cared nothing about the incarcerated and looked down on the guys as if they were no longer men due to their predicament.

Every month, Mr. Cooper took a trip over to the cell house where inmates were locked down in a room 23 hours a day. Today, he had to check on several guys on his case load. He strolled the hallway with his pad and stopped to observe the names on the doors. He stopped at one name on his list.

"Jeffrey Owen's," he yells. "Better hurry up before I change my mind."

"Yo!" Jeffrey hollers from the other side of the door. "Mr. Cooper, what's up, "Top Counselor."

"Don't know, you tell me. How you doing back here?"

Jeffrey's head is pressed against the door, he peers through the glass at the counselor and shakes his head pitifully. He was near defeat. "I really don't know Mr. Cooper. I'm doing... I guess."

"How long have you been back here?"

"It'll be three months Friday."

"You think you're ready to come back to the compound?"
"Yeah, I gotta get out of here Mr. Cooper."

"You know the Warden wanna ship your ass for that shit you pulled. You almost incited a fucking riot! I spoke to him personally and explained the issues you had. He told me you get one chance. You screw up again and I can guarantee you'll be out West before you could blink."

"I'm good now Mr. Cooper, but you know my situation. I been going through it. I needed this rest time in here though. I'm ready to come out now."

"Alright, I'll see if I get can get you out before count time. I'm glad the Islam Nation stepped in when they did. Shit could've got out of hand real fast. You're a good kid and I wanna see you leave here in one piece. Just lay it down for the last six months. By the way, I didn't know you were a member of Islam Nation. I don't have that on file."

"What Nation?"

"The Muslim brother's Nation that saved your ass!!"

"Oh, but I'm not. I don't even know any of the brothers. I went to a couple of their services, but I never really spoke to any of them. I'm not a member or anything like that."

"Well, it might not be a bad idea to join, at least until you leave," Mr. Cooper suggested. "I want you to come see me soon as you're out of here."

"Thanks Mr. Cooper!!"

CHAPTER 35

At 4 PM, inmates stood up to be counted. "Quiet down while we count fellas." The two officers on duty made their rounds. Count time was a big deal in prison. Interfering with it could mean an incident report that would likely land a prisoner in the hole.

"Count check! Mail call in 5!"

Brothers filled the hallways and prepared for the officer to pass out mail. Jeffrey jumped back on his bunk, unconcerned about mail call. His heart was filled with anger toward his **Maker** for what happen to Prince. How could anyone be so unfortunate? Just when he started to regain hope again, this happened. It was Friday and because he was fresh out of the hole, his telephone wouldn't be active until Monday. But that was the least of his worries. He didn't know what might happen as a result of the Gangster Disciple member he punched out. He thought about apologizing. After all, the guy only asked for a light. Jeffrey just lost it. He had just hung up the phone from hearing the news of Prince's shooting. Gangster Disciples rushed from every direction on the yard when witnessing the vicious attack on one of their own. The Islam Nation observed the disturbance and spotted Jeffrey and a couple of his boys surrounded by a little over 20 to 30 angry disciples.

Everyone acknowledged the Islam Nation. Brother Kihiem Muhammad, the Student Minister was one of the most respected men on the compound. A cat by the name of Chi Town out of Chicago was a spokesman for the Gd's. The two potential leaders stood for 15 minutes talking and negotiating a truce to not harm Jeffrey. He was adamant about protecting Jeffrey. The Gd's eventually backed down, but not before flashing Jeffrey their most menacing stare. Before Jeffrey could thank the Brother Minister for standing up for him, Jeffrey was summoned over the loudspeaker to report to the Lieutenant's office immediately. He was thrown in the hole under investigation for inciting a riot.

"Jeffrey, here cuz, you got mail." Joe hands him three letters.

"Damn my nig, you wild as hell!! You aight though?"

"Yeah…. Aye man, I gotta apologize for getting y'all caught up in that shit. Going through some things you know. But the hole was a bitch. My back still hurts."

"It's all good. We homies… If the shit would've popped off, me and you would've got punished. It had to be at least 30 of them niggas." Jeffrey shook his head, realizing how out of hand things could have gotten.

"Yeah mane, I'm just glad nothing happened. The shit was stupid anyway."

"Cuz, what's good with you and the Muslims? The niggas don't just step out there for anybody. I mean, they was ready to go all out for our ass."

Jeffrey had no idea. "I guess they just some good brothers. Where Scooter? I can't wait to see his crazy ass.

"You gone see that nigga in a minute. He gotta know you back on the pound. Well look homey, I'm gone break out and let you get your stuff together." They exchange pounds and Joe goes about his way. Jeffrey stares at the envelopes spread out over his bed. He sees Erica's name. The others was from Diane and the last was from…. **Shonda**.

"What a surprise," Jeffrey uttered to no one in particular. He tossed the other two aside and ripped open the letter from his sister. Before reading it, thoughts of Tiffany entered his mind. He couldn't believe she hadn't written to him, if just to see if he was okay. He figured if she could leave so easily, then she must have never been his girl from the start. An angry frown creased his forehead at just the thought of her.

Dear Jeffrey,

I hope you're okay in there. I have been calling your counselor, Mr. Cooper to see what happened. Britney and I are holding up considering... It seems like we're never going to catch a break. Something always come along to screw things up. Well, you probably know by now, the judge denied custody to Wanda because of what happened to Prince. She tried her best but the judge said she couldn't provide a safe environment for us.

I know you're upset about Prince, we all are. Everyone's tripping about it. I can remember the last time I talked to him. We had just left from visiting you. Everyone was so excited about the custody hearing. I still can't believe it's over just like that. Wanda still calls from time to time, but I can tell she's hurting. She said to tell you that she hasn't forgotten about us. She just needs some time to get herself together.

We love you Jeffrey. Don't be in their worrying about us. Things have to get better one day. I hate this place but at least we're not on the streets homeless. I guess things could always be a whole lot worse right? Brittney misses you and ask about you all the time. I don't know when we'll be able to come down there again but Wanda said probably next month sometime. Please call us, we need to hear from you. Times are hard but we are trying to be strong for you. So you do the same for us, okay? Your time is getting shorter every day that passes. It doesn't even seem like you been gone over a year. Well, keep your head up.

Love you, Erica

He felt better already. Upon opening another envelope, Jeffrey notice two other letters. One from Diane and the other from Black!!!! So anxious to hear from Black, he hurriedly unfolds the letter.

Jeffrey,

What up my nigga, I trust that you are holding strong. Ain't too much on this end. Damn player, it's been a long time since we kicked it but I always keep you in my thots. I talk to Diane all of the time. She keeps me posted on your situasion. She been holding me down to, she come down to see me every other month. I heard about Prince and I know you messed up about it. Still can't believe it myself.

I'm jive fucked up from still picturing his face on TV. That just goes to show you any batty can be touched. I feel bad about the letter I wrote and I know you read it. I can picture you now saying, "this nigga done lost his last damn mind." I folded under pressure my nigga, something I always thot I'd be ready for. Guess I won't strong as I thot I was . Prince ain't deserve what happened to him, he helped a lotta people. Anyway my nigga, how you doing? Heard you had your first taste of the hole. Don't feel bad, I spin 23 hours in a shit hole every day.

Damn, did you ever see all of this shit when we was kids, riding our bmx bikes? I miss my niggas. I be thinking about you and LA every day. Still can't believe my nigga gone. I still got the article on the whole shootout. My nigga went all out. I feel him tho, who the fuck wanna do life in prison? Death beats this shit any day. How Erica and Britney? Anyway take your time, I hear you aint got long before you hit the bricks... Be easy. Is Shorty girl still riding with you? I'm sure she is, you ain't got no time. All them sorry bitches bounced on me as soon as I got sentence. I don't blame them tho. Holla at your boy, don't be a stranger.

Black.... One

So happy to hear from his ace, Jeffrey read it over one more time before moving on to the next letter.

Dear son,

How are you baby? I hope you're doing well. Boy, when is they gone let you out that hole? Everything is alright here. I've been worrying myself to death about you. When you get this letter, write me straight back and let me know you're okay. I'm sorry to hear about you and Tiffa-

ny. I always thought she was a sweet girl but I see she just a another fast ass. Her butt ain't gone have no good luck leaving my baby in there like that. It's okay because you don't need her. You have plenty of people who love you.

I am sorry to hear about Prince. Didn't know him well, but LA talked about him all the time. It's sad what happened to him and that girl must've really loved him. I talk to Erica. They're doing fine. Well baby, I am sleepy but wanted you to know that I was thinking about you. Write me back or call when you are able.

Love, Diane

Jeffrey didn't receive this much mail in a while. He picked up Shonda's envelope about to read it, but was interrupted by Joe. "Here you go," Joe said, putting a huge pillow case beside Jeffrey's bunk.

"This is all your sweats and sneakers. It's a good thing I kept it. You already know the property dude be tripping. Oh yeah, they call chow too. You going out?"

"Hell yeah, I'm hungry as fuck!" Jeffrey said as he put all of his mail under the pillow.

"I'll just read this later." He jumps down from the top bunk and kicks off his shoes and bus clothes. After sliding on his sweat suit and a fresh pair of New Balance sneakers, he follows Joe out on to the compound to find Scooter. Soon as they reaches the door where prisoners are charging out the exit in rout to the dining hall, Jeffrey stops in his tracks!

"What the fuck is this?!" He mumbles under his breath at the mere sight of at least four Islam Nation brothers posted outside the housing unit, along with Chi Town and three other members of the Gd's.

"Fuck it, if it's on... Then let it be on," Joe says to Jeffrey, flashing a glimmering homemade blade just enough so that Jeffrey could see it. Jeffrey proceeds to walk out the door with Joe by his side. The guy he punched out was present and his ice grill game was on 1000. Jeffrey immediately prepares for round two but the Islam Nation intervened.

145

"Brotha Jeffrey," the sharply dressed figure greets upon approaching Jeffrey. "Glad to see you back with us." After shaking the youngster's hand, Akim nods over to the Gd's. "Jeffrey, the Islam Nation is about peace. We don't want our brothers fighting amongst each other." Akim eyes Jeffrey seriously. "You owe this brother an apology."

The youngster turned to Joe, then glanced over at the four Gd's. Focusing his attention back on Akim, he spoke. "You right, I do owe him an apology."

Everyone was impressed to see a young man like Jeffrey set aside his pride. Akim smiled, then escorted Jeffrey over toward the gang members with Joe close behind. The men talked for a while and Jeffrey explained all of the events that led up to the incident. Everybody shook hands and parted ways, but before Jeffrey could walk off, Akim called him back.

"The Student Minister wants you to attend the next service at the end of the month. He'll be speaking and wants you to be there."

"Alright, I'll be there brother," replied Jeffrey. Akim began to walk off when Jeffrey thanks him.

"Don't thank us brother. We're just doing our duty. You can show appreciation by being there on time." With that said, Jeffrey and Joe makes their way to the compound.

CHAPTER 36

On the second floor of Jeffrey's unit, down a long stretch of hall-way, past the officers station, there was a room inmates referred to as the BOOM BOOM ROOM. It was located directly in the very back of the housing unit and officers never went back there unless it was count time. There wasn't but one recreation officer, so the track was closed. The yard was too small and there was nowhere to smoke without their spot being blown. Jeffrey, Scooter and Joe headed back to the unit.

Big Todd had been doing time since the late 80s. His cell was directly across from the **BOOM BOOM ROOM**. Whenever Scooter would stop by to visit, Todd would put his cell mate out and make him watch for the police. Scooter, Jeffrey and Joe sat in the semi dim cell with the big homey. He loved whenever younger cats came into the system because they still had connections to the streets. Scooter was so thrilled to have Jeffrey back, that he already had three blunts twisted and waiting. Big Todd had two gallons of homemade hooch for them to sip on while they passed the weed back and forth, blowing each other shotguns.

The group took turns telling stories about sexing chicks and old shootouts. Jeffrey was feeling woozy after his second cup of wine. For the most part, everyone had interesting stories, but Big Todd always manage to take the story telling to another level. For instance, no one wanted to hear about bloody shank fights and boys getting their asses taken. The in-cents burned strong to mask the odor of the weed as the guys joked about Jeffrey hitting the boy over nothing.

It was the only spot where they could chill back, enjoy their high and put problems to rest, if only for the moment.... Jeffrey was so blitzed he thought the walls were moving. Feeling sick on the stomach from a cup too many, he excused himself and told the boys he had to lay down. They clowned him and said he couldn't hang.

When he left, Scooter was sparking up the fourth blunt.

Back on his bunk, Jeffrey closed his eyes, smiling as he remembered the letter under his pillow, anxious to hear what Shonda had to say. Jeffrey sat up slowly, fumbling through the mail, wishing in his heart that the letter was from Tiffany.

"Damn, whoever dude is must be fucking her real good to make her just say fuck me," he thought as he focused on the letter in front of him.

Dear Jeffrey,

Hey boy, I hope you doing alright. Me, well I'm good. Mom asks about you, she said hi. I know you're surprised to hear from me. I've been wanting to write you but I knew how you felt about Tiffany. I heard you two ain't together now and I hope you ain't tripping over no broad anyway.

I have so many things I want to talk about but right now, I'm just gone keep it simple. I just want you to know I'm here for you whenever you need a friend or someone to talk to. I miss seeing your face and can't wait until you come home. I hate seeing you locked up. I spoke to Black a couple months ago. Him and mom talked for a while. Jeffrey we've been friends for a long time now. I have something I need to say that I've been holding in for too long, but I'll wait until the time is right.

Don't be in their stressing about Tiffany ass either. Just give it some time, she'll regret ever leaving you like that. Call me so I can hear your voice. I can't believe you ain't called me yet. I have to go now. I'm on my lunch break. You better write back!

Always, Shonda

"Damn!" Jeffrey muttered as the lights cut out. He thought about Tiffany as he laid there in darkness. As much as he tried to hate her for what she'd done, he just couldn't. Something inside of him still loved her deeply. Aside from his mother, Jeffrey had never loved anyone that way. Shame it took him to go to prison to realize it. His heart was caught in the middle and losing her was like being ripped to pieces. And though Jeffrey desperately longed for the sound of her voice, somehow he knew he'd have to find the strength to let go. It killed him to imagine her sexing another man the way she did him.

In the darkness, he pictured her tender flesh being caressed by another. The more he thought about her, the more he realized he could never go back to her. He never even considered the possibility of Tiffany being out of his life. Jeffrey recited the words from an unfinished poem he was in the process of writing:

"Love is like a faucet, it turns off and on... Sometimes when you think it's on, it has turned off and gone."

The Ghost

CHAPTER 37

The police arrested Wanda, charging her with manslaughter for the guy she shot dead in the middle of the street. The few times she visited the shooting range with Prince had paid off. It wasn't the plan, her man was in trouble and she reacted the way she always told Prince she would. Her only regret was that she wasn't able to act sooner. Prince made her purchase the registered gun, telling her that it may come in handy one day.

Years ago before going to prison, Prince used to tell her how envious dudes were of him and added that they may even try to use her as bait to get to him. She always had questions. *'Why would they want me? I don't have anything.'* He'd simply smile at her innocent face. "*Girl, you got a lot to learn about this game. You don't gotta have shit. You the closest person to me and niggas know that and will use that to their advantage.*" Prince was adamant as he schooled her and she never missed an opportunity to soak up game. He also told her to keep her eyes in the rear view and never come straight home.

After receiving a message from his secretary, Mr. Rockafield was on the first flight to Richmond Virginia. Residence of Mosby heard about Wanda's arrest and stormed to the police precinct, demanding that she be released. Several witnesses were willing to testify on her behalf. And the District Attorney already knew the story from reports submitted to his office on the shooting. Wanda had to sit because of the weekend but the lawyer had her out on bail first thing Monday morning.

The next few months would pass by slowly for Wanda. Prince was the last person she expected to fall victim to a vicious attack. Little Pernell was devastated and asked questions she couldn't answer. Although she was hurting, she still managed to be patient, choosing her words carefully when talking to her son about his father. It had been three months since they left Richmond for their Atlanta estate. Wanda found so much peace there and was often angry at herself for not pushing for them to leave sooner.

Their house was worth a couple million, it was the fairytale life she'd always dreamed of having. Standing in the wide bedroom window over looking their spacious back yard, Wanda watches as Pernell and her sister's children run around playing chase. Her sister Lisa had agreed to come down and stay with her for a while to help out with Pernell. Changing her focus from the window to the bedroom, Wanda made her way slowly over to the bed. "Hey baby, it's about time you got up. Let me help you."

Awakening from a deep sleep, Prince yawns as his queen comes into focus. "What's up baby." Bottles of meds were on the night stand next to him.

"Are you hungry? I made your favorite just the way you like it."

Wanda adjusted his bed so that he could eat his meal comfortably. The aroma from the food was to die for. "Damn, I gotta get use to this shit. Thanks baby, smells good. I'll get to it in a minute. Help me out this bed." Blood loss from the shooting left Prince 20 pounds lighter. Wanda lifted his frail body, placing him up right in his wheelchair. Rolling himself in front of a huge mirror, Prince stared at his reflection in disgust. "I can't believe this shit! Look at me... How you gone love a nigga like this?"

Wanda saunters over to him and kneels down so that they are looking one another directly in the eyes.

"Listen to me... I love you Prince! I don't give a damn about you being paralyzed. I still got my husband and Pernell still got his father." Tears stream down her face as she continue. "You almost died that day Prince. Nothing will ever change my feelings for you. You are still the only man for me and I'm never leaving your side. Just let me take care of you boo!" She take his hand in hers and caresses it, lifting it to her lips for a kiss. "Don't take my word for it, just watch and see. I ain't going nowhere."

CHAPTER 38

Tiffany was the hottest young thing in the projects. Looking at her, one would never guess that she was only 17. She had breasts of a full grown woman, standing at 5'5" with a knockout physique. She was a cutie and knew it. It was because of her that a lot of cats envied Jeffrey. He was the first to rock her world. Jeffrey was far from a baller but an expert at sexing a woman.

When brothers went to prison, it created the perfect opportunity for that guy to go after that female they'd been clocking for years. *One man's downfall, was another man's come up.* Even so called friends became predators. However, the fact that Jeffrey was half crazy and wouldn't be gone long, kept them at bay, only lusting.

Eco had grown to hate Tiffany. Every time he saw her and Rakee together, he got the itch to pull out his strap and blast on the car. He couldn't get over the phony love she portrayed when Jeffrey was home. He thought about all the times she and Jeffrey were together, then how she flipped on his boy the minute he took a fall.

Rakee parked directly in front of Tiffany's apartment, cut off the head lights and made a quick call to Tiffany. He peered through the tinted windows of his brand new seven series BMW at the figures across the street. He retrieved the Desert Eagle from the floor, secured it on his waist and made his exit. The last thing he needed was a confrontation over a broad. Tiffany was waiting in the doorway as Rakee walked up, momentarily distracted from the intimidating group across the street. No static this time, Rakee entered the apartment with no problem.

Inside, Tiffany stood in the middle of the floor pouting like a little girl. Her mother Gloria walked by flashing Rakee a mischievous grin. "You in trouble," She whispered over her shoulder and walked up the stairs.

"Happy Birthday!!! Oh damn, you ain't fucking with your boy today?"

"Where you been at? You know I wanted to spend my birthday with you."

Rakee put on his most serious expression. "I had something important I had to take care of."

"But,"

"You need to calm your ass down! Now, I ain't saying that shit was more important than you, but it was important. I told you shorty, I gotta a lot going on. I didn't call back because I knew I was gone see you tonight."

He pulled her into his arms. "You know damn well I won't gone forget your birthday."

"How many girls do you have?" Tiffany ask out of the blue. Suddenly her phone rings as she stand there waiting on a response. She was not going to answer, but he insisted that she do. It was Jeffrey calling. Tiffany picks up the phone and quickly slams it back down and turns off the ringer!!

Rakee shakes his head at her. "Jeffrey again? You see, that could be me you hanging the phone up on."

She'd heard the sermon before. She rolled her eyes and sucked her teeth, clearly a indication that she didn't care to hear his bullshit.

"Are you going to answer my question or what?"

"Let me explain something to you first." He let go of a huge sigh. "I never told you to leave dude. I was perfectly satisfied with us just being cool and for real, I wanted you to still bid with cuz. Seriously now, how you expect me to cut off all my ties with hoes just because you left him? I'm not trying to hurt your feelings, but I gotta keep it 100 with you. I got hoes coming at me everywhere I go and of course I deal with other girls. Shit, you left that nigga, I know damn well you'll leave me. Don't cry Tiffany... I gotta let you know the real instead of sitting here faking with you... Only a sucker could ask a broad to leave a nigga like that while he down and that just ain't me."

"You didn't ask me to do nothing. It was my choice." He took Tiffany's hand and lead her over to the couch where they both sat. "Regardless though, I'm not cool with the fact that I may be the reason you left him. "

"Rakee.. It's my birthday. Right now I just need a lil love, do you think you can handle that"

"You ain't even see your birthday present." His words brought an instant smile to her face. She resembled a little girl.

"Where is it?" He pointed to the gifts laying on the couch. She rushed across the room to pick up the Victoria Secrets bag. Rakee smiles at Tiffany's reaction to the lavender G-string as she stares at the lingerie confused. Tiffany turns to face Rakee, who throw up his hands in surrender.

"Okay okay, I kind of bought that gift for myself. I gotta see you in them motherfuckers!"

At the sound of her mother's voice, Tiffany tosses the panties back in the Victoria Secrets bag. She sat on Rakee's lap and wraps her arms around his neck. "Are you staying with me tonight?" Asked Tiffany in a long and drawn out tone.

"Hell no, get your shit, you staying with me. Throw something on real quick, I'll be in the car."

The Ghost

CHAPTER 39

Crack head Faye was tall and medium build, lugging a donkey ass. Every project had at least one trick who had sampled all of the dealers. Back in her day, Faye was a beauty. Her first son was by Prince's crew member, Big Weed. Since the day he received his life sentence, she spiraled downhill, messing around with young dope pushers who showed her no respect. Prince couldn't believe how drastically she had changed when he returned to the streets. Faye had gone from prom queen to crack fiend in just a matter of years.

Prince took care of Big Weed's sons like they were his own. At first, he used to give her money for the boys but that soon changed after learning from the streets that she was smoking. He'd give her money for school clothes and whatever else the children needed, but Faye would go and spend the cash with one of the street dealers. As the years passed, her condition worsened, the drugs began to eat away at her physical appearance. Whenever Faye didn't have money, she had no problem getting down on her knees. Eventually, she grew accustomed to the junky life until all she did was trick for a fix.

After Prince left the Avenue, the up and coming hustlers turned her apartment into a trap spot where they cooked and bagged up drugs. It was also a hideaway whenever police bum rushed the block. But LA and Black were the first to turn out her apartment. When they were physically out there, hustlers weren't allowed to even hang around their setup. Faye was crazy about those two and still talked about how well they treated her. She never had to ask for anything because they made sure she had all that she needed. Food was there for the children, the bills were paid on time and other fiends hated on her because she always smoked the best coke.

Now she was forced to deal with low budget hustlers like Eco and his boys. They were cheap and would make her do some of the wildest stunts for a bump. Eco and the rest of his buddies would be in their smoking marijuana, stoned out of their minds, telling Faye to do things like, perform a hand stand while she smoked crack. She had been a star in track and field in earlier days and was still very flexible. There was nothing in the world funnier than a crack head stunting for a fix.

In the hood, she was a crack head superstar. Nobody disrespected her verbally and definitely not physically. Messing around with Faye, was asking for a crucial beat down. The hood didn't play when it came to Faye. Lil Mikey shot another fiend for blacking Faye's eye one night. Although he lived, he never thought once about snitching out the young thug. The fiends were terrified of the hustlers in Grey Stone.

Eco sat in Fay's small living room with Marlo, watching her dance nude in the middle of the floor. Her body was still tempting, despite her habit. The room grew hazy from the weed smoke as she danced provocatively to the music. Her ass shook invitingly while she caressed her firm nipples. The two watched her with lustful eyes, scheming on taking her in the middle of the floor. Faye kneels in front of Eco after noticing the bulge in his jeans. She ran her hand across his hard member and attempted to unzip his jeans when an expected knock at the door brought everything to a screeching halt.

"Let them motherfuckers knock mane!" Marlo said raising to his feet. He stood directly behind her thick frame, squeezing her tender butt while she proceeded to stuff her mouth with Eco's meat."

Banging on the door persist until it becomes a distraction and the so called menage is over before it could even start. "Who the fuck is it?" Eco barks while quickly zipping up his paints. Faye grabs her clothes and hurries upstairs with Marlo behind her. Eco swings the door open! "What the fuck mane! God damn, let a nigga live!!"

Mango, another young hustler from the projects, stand before him hyped up. "Yo, I won't go fuck with you because I knew you was in here tricking, but you gotta see this shit!!!"

Eco peek out the door and glance up the block. "Nigga, I know damn well you see 5 0 on the block. Fuck you out here banging for?"

"They locking up your girl Tiffany.... Smart ass nigga!!"

The youngster broke out after passing the info to Eco. People were lingering around everywhere and four police cars were parked right outside Tiffany's apartment. Her mother cried as the poor teenager came out in handcuffs. Tiffany's bloody shirt was ripped and her hair stood on the top of her head as if someone had tried to pull it out of her scalp. Her friends stood in the streets, some of them weeping while Tiffany was escorted by officers to the patrol car. The scene was jam packed with elderly, dealers and children. Eco stood back from a distance in an attempt to stay clear of the police.

"Damn, I wonder what the hell she got herself into," he said as the patrol car drove off with Tiffany in the back seat. Standing near Tiffany's Honda Accord, Eco spots her friend Trina with a group of girls. Trina saw him approaching and left her girls to meet him.

"What happened to your girl?" Asked Eco. "Did she get into a fight or something?"

Trina simply shakes her head as tears well in the corner of her eyes. "We was all fighting."

"With who though?"

"I can't believe this shit," Trina was furious. "I tried to stop her."

"Stop her from doing what?"

"She cut Rakee's baby mama!"

"Oh shit.." Eco seemed to be shocked. "You can't be serious."

She went on to tell him how it all went down at Natural Motion, Beauty Salon on Hull Street. According to Trina, the two of them were simply sitting in the salon minding their business.

"Tiffany was already upset after bumping into his baby mama but she started popping slick shit about Rakee.... *What he did for her and her daughter.* Tiffany just snapped. She had all our asses fighting up in that motherfucker. We beat that bitches ass! I don't know why she pulled a razor out. She even cut the girl who owned the shop. We got the hell out there after that. The police wouldn't even let Tiffany change her shirt."

"Damn, well God don't like ugly. She shouldn't have carried my man, J that way."

"I don't know what that nigga put on my girl," Trina exclaimed sadly.

Marlo finally walked up with a wide grin on his face. "Tiffany got locked up, what happened?"

Eco couldn't help from laughing at his boy. "Damn nigga, where the fuck you been at?"

"I had to get this stress up off of me cuz. **Faye say get at her though.**

CHAPTER 40

The master bedroom was a remarkable sight, 850 ft. of pure elegance and relaxation. A 20 inch soft tan leather ottoman lined the side wall adjacent to a king size Victorian style sleeper, fitted with black satin sheets and a down comforter set, pillow cases to match, monogrammed with Prince's initials. A Van Hansen perfume and cologne dispenser sat on top of a plush ivory Berber carpet, containing 80 different selections at the press of a button. A mounted wooden cabinet revealed a hidden Clarion 50 inch TV, equipped with a five speaker Dolby surround sound at the remotes request. The viewer had a choice between satellite TV or a DVD selection the size of Blockbuster's videos. The highlight was the bathroom. The couple would often sit in the 50' jet whirlpool Jacuzzi, press a button and watch the ceiling open up to a clear starlight sky.

The serene Atlanta night sky was surely something to write home about. Wanda laid cuddled up next to Prince, wide awake while gazing up at the stars. The moon was full and her surroundings was peaceful. She dreamed about the day when she'd finally be able to exhale and recline next to the person she loved unconditionally. For so many years, she'd fantasize about being Prince's wife and the two of them growing old together in their dream house.

The accident had only brought them closer together. And naturally, she would often have thoughts of one day becoming tired of pushing around a wheelchair. But her love for Prince overcame and dismissed any doubts. Teardrops fell from Wanda's eyes onto the pillow as she relived the moment in her mind of Prince's shooting. She felt blessed to still have him lying next to her, in spite of his condition. Any way she could have the O G was fine with her. Wanda embraced her man tightly, kissing him gently on the neck, whispering the words, "I love you," softly in his ear.

Prince knew it was morning time when he felt the hot sun beaming in on his face. "Shit," he cursed Wanda for leaving the ceiling open then grabbed the control, yawning and stretching out over the enormous bed. He thrust at his lifeless legs, then peers down at them. The mere sight of the shriveled sticks makes him grimace.

Several months had passed, but he still found it hard to believe, hoping to wake up one morning to find that it was all a bad dream.

"Can't win them all." He uttered, reflecting back to when he'd killed a guy for Justice. The more he thought about his attacker, the more he realized that he couldn't even be mad. If the shoe was on the other foot, he would have done the same.

Wanda gave him great strength. After she left the first time, he swore that he would never love again, but the heart had a mind of its own. When love called, the heart could become a stubborn organ, the mind's adversary. He often got lost gazing into her eyes and he wondered if she still loved him the same... Had things changed between them?

"Only time would tell," he said finally sitting up in bed. He thought day in and day out about the dedication she had shown, laying down her life without hesitation. Rockafield had been able to talk the DA into dismissing her charges the week before. Yet and still, Wanda's demeanor did not seem to change. It was clear that her concern was not the penalty she'd pay for coming to her man's aid, but rather making sure he knew how strongly she felt for him, and to what extent she would go to prove this.

Prince was back to his old self, gaining nearly all of his weight back. He was as strong as an ox, determined not to waste away in that wheelchair. He worked out constantly in the small gym in his basement with the assistance of a ***private trainer/therapist***. The aroma of Wanda's cooking filled his nostrils, giving his stomach an instant voice. One at a time, he slowly lifted his legs until both were hanging off the bed. After securing himself in his wheelchair, Prince slid his feet inside his Gucci slippers, then rolled out into the bathroom to wash up. Months after his accident, he had two elevators installed. It was a short ride downstairs and when the doors opened, Pernell was standing right there waiting to greet his father.

"Daddy, about time you woke up. Mama fixed breakfast!"

"Is that right? What did she fix little man?"

The boy hugged and kissed his father, "steak, eggs, and, ummm........ Potatoes."
"Man that sounds good. You ready to eat?"

"We've been waiting on you dad!" Prince laughed at how grown his boy had become.

Wanda walks up, "hey baby." She kisses his lips. "How you feeling this morning?" Prince glances up at her, then over at Pernell, making his way to the breakfast table.

"Good girl. What about yourself?"

Her face flushes with joy. He had never seen her happier. "Couldn't be better. Come on and eat."

The three of them gathered around the table. After they bowed their heads, Wanda proceeded with the grace, thanking God for the food and her family.

Prince was hungry and his son snickered at him. "Slow down dad," he said. Wanda smiled proudly at her two favorite men as she sliced the tender steak, popping a piece into her mouth.

"Did you hear anything else about Tiffany," asked Prince.

"I knew it was something I had to tell you. Chelle say they gone give that girl some time."

"Who is Tiff-" Pernell started to ask before his mother shot an evil glare his way. "What I tell you about getting into grown folks business."

Minutes pass quietly, "mom, I finished eating. Can I go play the game?"

"Go ahead boy. Take your plate up first."

"Okay. Dad, you still gone play pool with me? Remember you promised last night?"

"I'll be in there soon as I finished eating and talking to your mama. Better have your game face on too!"

Pernell smiles and disappears into the basement. Prince looks over at Wanda. "Now go on, what you say about her?"

"Oh, that girl got four charges and Chelle say she gone do some years. I can't believe she cut a girl over some dude."

Prince sat back. "Damn, she was a nice girl too."

"How Jeffrey sound when you talk to him?"

A smile appeared on Prince's face. "He holding it down. That's a strong young nigga. He sounds good to me. When I brought Tiffany's situation up, he ain't even seem to be phased at all. I think he gonna be alright."

"Well, that's good. I wanna take the girls down to see him next week if that's fine with you. I'll try to visit her when I go down to Richmond next week."

"Alright, go ahead and holla at him, he ain't got but two months to go."

"I'll call Diane tomorrow. You finished eating?"

"Yeah, I'm going to shoot a couple games with Pernell. He swear he can beat me now that I'm in a wheelchair." Prince takes a deep breath. "Damn woman, you did your thing with that steak. It was all that baby!"

"Glad you liked it. After you finish with Pernell, I'll give you a message alright."

Prince nods in silence and backs up from the table. Wanda pops the last piece of steak in her mouth and stands up to clean off the table. Pernell is already practicing when his father rolls up. The kid concentrates on his next shot, missing the whole by inches.

The O G smiles, "I see you done step your game up. Ready for me?"

"Yup, I'm ready to whip your butt!"

"Rack 'em then. You don't really think you can beat your daddy, now do you?"

"Come on old man," replied Pernell with mountains of confidence. Prince grabs his favorite stick from the wall and waits for his son to rack the balls.

"Daddy," the kid calls out and father and son shares eye contact. "Why do you have to be in that wheel chair?"

Prince was totally unprepared for the question and thought carefully before responding. "Come over here and let me talk to you." Pernell put the stick on the table and comes to stand before his father. "Jump up there." He quickly hops up on the edge of the table.

"Son, sometimes things happen in life that are hard to understand. I was shot and the bullets from the gun messed up my spine, causing me to be paralyzed."

"So that mean you ain't gone be able to play football with me?"

"No son, daddy ain't playing no football like this. It's lots of other things we can still do though. Don't be thinking your daddy helpless, because he in a wheelchair. You know Pernell, it could always be worse. Daddy could have died that day. So even though I'm paralyzed, we still have to be thankful right? Remember what mama said?"

"Dad, why would someone shoot you?"

Prince hated lying to his son and knew if he didn't help Pernell understand, this conversation would arise again in the future.

"I'm gone tell you this one time and then I'm gone whip you in pool, OK?"

"OK."

"I did something real bad a long time ago. And it came back on me, understand?"

Pernell nods his head in conformation.

"Tell me what I mean then, since you understand."

The boy looks at his father crazily. "You saying when you do wrong, it comes back on you... Right?"

Prince grins, "smart boy. Now come on and let daddy beat you right quick."

"In your dreams old man," the boys says with a smile.

CHAPTER 41

Tiffany received two counts on each charge of assault with a deadly weapon and vandalism for tearing up the girls beauty salon. Detective Daniels didn't even recognize the pretty face as officers hauled her into the station but knew for certain that they had cross paths before. After leaving the precinct, Tiffany's face bothered him so much that he turned around and headed back to find out her name.

He knew exactly who she was the minute he saw her name. After reading the charges with a smirk on his face, he stood outside the interrogation room and observed her for a few moments through the glass. Apart of him pitied her, but the other half enjoyed every second of her discomfort. He eventually signaled for the officer to give him a few minutes alone with her. Tiffany's head lifted up from the table as the door opened and Detective Daniels walked in with a shit faced look. At least that's what Tiffany thought of the smile plastered on his smug face.

Daniels started to take a seat next to her on the table but quickly decided against it after reflecting back over the incident with Black.

"Tiffany, isn't this a surprise?" He tossed the charge papers on the table. "I see you've gotten yourself in one hella mess."

"What do you want?"

"Nothing really. Just wanted to see how you were holding up. I know you're pretty tough from the charges you took for Jeffrey. The only difference this time is.... You're going to prison. How's Jeffrey doing these days? He should be coming home sometime soon right. It's a shame you won't be here to greet him."

Tiffany was dying inside and the last thing she needed to hear was Jeffrey's name. In tears, she desperately tried to tune out the detective's lecture.

"Can you please just leave me alone?" Tiffany pleaded with Daniels. He grabbed the papers and headed out the door. Before leaving, he turned to inform Tiffany that he'd be present at her arraignment.

Rakee despised Tiffany and didn't want to see or talk to her. He went past the apartment and spoke to her mother and explained to Gloria how Tiffany was wrong for her actions. He offered to pay for the lawyer and bail, but made it perfectly clear that he wanted nothing else to do with her. The arraignment was a mess. When Judge Thomas Munsey denied bail because the charges were too serious, Tiffany broke out in tears. Her attorney David McCauley reminded the court that she was still in school and that it was her first offense. Tiffany's eyes remained glued on the prosecutor and detective while her attorney did everything he could to convince the judge. After the hearing was over, McCauley went to visit his client in the bullpen.

"Did you know the detective sitting behind the prosecutor?"

When she said yes, the attorney explained to her the part detective Daniels played in the judge denying bail. "Tiffany do you understand that you're facing over 10 years and that's just for the two attempted murders?"

He looked through sympathetic eyes at Tiffany. "Now I have spoken with the District Attorney and he's willing to drop all charges if you plead guilty to one count of assault which carries a five-year minimum."

"How much time will I have to do then?"

The lawyer took a deep breath. "3 1/2 years tops." Tiffany was devastated. She didn't want to do a day!!! H–1 in the Richmond city jail housed women only. The first couple of weeks nearly killed Tiffany. She had never seen anything like what was going on in jail. Females were out of control and fought daily with one another. She hadn't slept for eight hours the entire month and a half. Chicken heads filled the tier and gossiped from day until they shut their eyes. They talked about the streets a lot... The usual, who's sexing who; the murder rate among other things.

The girls didn't exercise much. Jail was the perfect place for crack heads and dope addicts to regain their humanity. They would come in looking like something similar to the living dead, face sunk in from the huge amounts of crack consumed. Dope addicts suffered horribly when first arriving. They vomited every day. Tiffany only talked to a few girls she knew from the streets. One had to be careful when choosing friends inside that rat hole. And pretty young girls like Tiffany was instant prey for the many lesbians on the tier.

Tiffany's mind drifted back and forth from Rakee to Jeffrey. She knew that Rakee would be upset with her but she never expected to be cut off completely. He did accept her calls, but no letters and definitely no visits. She cried for two weeks, thinking that she was going to die inside. But as those weeks turned into months and there was still no word from him, she gave up. Jeffrey suddenly took total control over her thought process. Now she understood how he felt, and she even apologized over and over in her head for turning her back on him. She felt like the biggest fool in history for fighting over someone who didn't belong to her. And now, here she was locked up, about to do years while Rakee went about his life.

It was 11 pm when Tiffany stepped into the steamy hot shower. Stripping herself bare, she slipped under the warm current, letting out a sigh of relief. Two minutes of showering, she began to hear groaning sounds followed by women giggling. By now, she'd learned to mind her business in the shower. Looking at another nude female could send out the wrong signal. She could see what appeared to be two girls making out in the corner. Tiffany quickly rinsed off.

"Come on honey, there's room for one more," Eva offered. Both girls were proud lesbians. Patricia says. "Ain't nobody up but us girl. We ain't gone say nothing. I bet you got some sweet stuff, come let me taste."

Tiffany didn't respond, she hurriedly grabbed her towel and left out the shower dripping wet. Eva laughed at the nervous chick before popping one of Patricia's perky tits in her mouth. Not fazed by Tiffany's interruption, they resumed their freak session as Eva dipped a finger into Patricia's wetness.

Now that the shoe was on the other foot, she knew exactly how her man was feeling all alone. If only she could have had patients. The conversation with her mother had been haunting her ever since her arrest and she wished she had listened.... "Choose the person who love you, not the one you think you love."

She closed her eyes.

CHAPTER 42

Jeffrey completed the study guide class and was now a member of the Islam Nation. Kihiem Muhammad had been sticking to the youngster ever since his speech. Never had Jeffrey heard someone put it down the way brother minister put it down at service the other day. He found himself drawn to this guy in some strange way that he couldn't quite understand. Kihiem Muhammad was wise beyond years and understood the struggle like no other.

They had become the best of friends and spent lots of time together. Between him preparing for his release and his new workout schedule, he hardly ever saw Scooter and Joe. Jeffrey still wrote poems and songs, still hoping to one day put his talents to some use.

For the first time in his life, Jeffrey felt free, able to focus again. Tiffany didn't exist in his mind anymore and he started to feel his strength coming back. Although he had yet to find his purpose, he knew he had one. Flashbacks of the dreadful night in Charlottesville was still fresh in his mind as though it had just happen yesterday. The shootout with LA and how that whole ordeal unfolded, not to mention the two slugs that unsuccessfully got caught in his vest. Thanks to LA of course. He could remember vividly, LA strapping the bullet proof vest on his chest, totally unconcerned with his own safety. He gave Jeffrey his only vest and ended up possibly dying because of it. But LA wouldn't have had it any other way. What a friend.

It was a big day for sports fans at F. C. I. Lexington. Inmates gathered in clusters on the yard for the seasons last game. The two best teams on the compound were facing off and Trick Dave had finally met his

171

match. A cat by the name of Lil Cee out of Baltimore, was said to have a superb game as well, and had been waiting to finally play against his long time rival. The compound had been anticipating this game for the longest. Bookies were out in full force, ready to bet whatever on Trick Dave. A few inmates dipped off to the track for a quick chronic break before the game.

The yard was so packed that extra officers were summoned by the institutions top officials in case drama unfolded. Both teams formed a layup line to warm up for the battle. Trick Dave talked trash to the sideline, telling them to have his money ready after the game. When the ball tipped off, all eyes focused on the blacktop.

After a couple hard fouls, Trick Dave stopped going to the rim, switching his attack to crisp jumpers from the field. Coming down the court, a team member throws Lil Cee an alley hoop from the top of the key. He cradles it with one hand, slamming a spectacular dunk on two opponents. Trick Dave's team is down by three with a couple of minutes to go. He catches the ball on the wing, dribbles straight pass the weak defense. Taking the ball up, he fakes a layup with his right, then switches to his left, sinking the bucket and drawing the foul. The referee blows the whistle, sending the star to the line for a three-point play.

After hitting the shots and tying the score, Trick Dave glanced over toward the sideline at some of the guys that he'd bet.

"Ya'll niggas look like money. Get that paper together champ, it's about to be game time!!!"

With only 15 seconds left, players from both teams scramble to sink the winning basket. As the final seconds ticks off the clock, a buzzer sounds and the game goes into overtime. Jeffrey sat on the bench and observed the game while he waited for his mentor to show up. Exhausted from pumping iron, he guzzles half of the water in his cooler. Brother Kihiem walks up and grins at the youngster as Jeffrey began complaining about his swollen biceps. But in the process of Jeffrey rambling, he notice this awful sad look about Kihiem. He could sense that something was on his mind.

Prison was a strange place. Just being there was enough to drive a man insane, let alone the daily bullshit one had to endure. Kihiem had done a lot of time and still had a long ways to go. They had gotten tight and Jeffrey was on his way out. It was bitter sweet, Jeffrey understood. Jeffrey tapped his leg as they came to sat on a nearby bench. "What's with you my brother?" Jeffrey smiles to try and ease the tension. "I'm just so proud of you man. I see your growth and it makes me proud. You've come a long way and I believe that you're going to be alright out there.... On another note though, I need to speak with you about something...."

At this point, Jeffrey was certain that whatever it was bothering Brother Minister, it had to be important. But as he attempted to speak, "this is really har-"

"RECALL!!!"

It was the call for all inmates to report back to their housing unit. The damn thing blasted over the loud speaker totally disrupting Kihiem's train of thought.

Kihiem sighed and eyed Jeffrey, managing to squeeze out a tight smile as he looked impatiently down at his watch and swears. "I didn't know it was this late." Again, Jeffrey observes this sudden urgency in his face but Kihiem's smile put him at ease.

"You know what, some other time Jeffrey. No big deal."

"Okay cool."

"You almost there, wow... Three weeks to go!!" Judging from his excitement, one would've thought Kihiem Muhammad was the one getting released. Jeffrey laughed with his new friend but the sadness in Kihiem's eyes didn't go unnoticed. He hated the fact that his friend had 10 more years left on his sentence. Guys rushed the gate in an effort to be first in line for the shower. Joe was waiting out front smoking on a Black and Mild when Jeffrey walked up.

"What up brother Muhammad."

"Oh, so you got jokes."
"Damn nigga, them weights swelling yo ass up. You gone make me have to come out of retirement."

He and Jeffrey doubled over in laughter as his comedian friend flexed his bird chest. "I think you got mail too."

Jeffrey entered the unit and headed straight to the officers station to retrieve his mail. He produced an ID for the officer and in return, he was handed an envelope. Jeffrey simply grinned and shook his head upon seeing the return address and a letter from Tiffany inside the envelope sent by her mother. She couldn't just send mail straight to an institution so Tiffany had to get her mom to three way the mail to Jeffrey. He wasn't even happy to hear from her.

Scooter walked up as Jeffrey was about to hop the stairs. "What up nicca!!! Holla at your boy."

Jeffrey dabbed his man up, then he flashed Tiffany's letter in Scooter's face.

"Oh so she got at you, huh. But I told you she would, though."

"I'll check you later," said Jeffrey.

"You know we gotta kick it before you bounce!"

"Soon as I finish reading this letter."

Jeffrey finally made it to his bunk and took a seat. He got into the letter before anyone else could interrupt.

Dear Jeffrey,

How are you doing? Find I hope. As for me, well I know you

found out by now what happened. Jeffrey I know you are disappointed with me and you should be. I sit here on my bed every night, day dreaming about how wrong I was. I don't have any excuses, I was weak and there's not a day that goes by that I don't regret it.

I'm writing to apologize and hope you'll somehow find it in your heart to forgive me. I can't believe two years have passed. So what are your plans when you get home? I've been locked up three months and I'm about to die!!

I don't know how I'm gonna do 3 1/2 years. It's so disgusting in here. Girls diking and shit. I feel so lonely in this place Jeffrey. I just wish I could hear your voice. I know you probably hate my guts but please try to understand. I don't think I can do this time without you. I never stop loving you. It's just.... I can't even explain it.... I needed you Jeffrey and you wasn't there!!!! The guy I was seeing just said all the right things. I don't hear from anyone, none of my sorry friends write. They won't even come and see me and I'm only 10 minutes away.

Jeffrey I don't care how crazy I may sound. I need you, don't you still love me????????

Everyone deserves a second chance. Three years of my life gone over nothing. Now, here I am asking you to bid with me. Life is crazy but I guess I brought all of this on myself. I don't want to talk you to death but I need a letter... I'm glad you're coming home. Don't wait too long to write back, bye.

Love always and forever... Tiffany

The Ghost

CHAPTER 43

Five 0!!" Three young adolescents at the corner yelled at the top of their lungs. It was the (jump out squad) the police and they came in full force, storming in from all three entrances. Several officers crept through the woods, catching a group of dealers in the middle of a high stakes crap game. Four squad cars parked in the middle of the street, jumped out to chase down a couple of young flat footers.

Police knew when to chase a dealer and when not to. Some dude's in the projects just refused to be caught. There were many Trap Houses to hide in and the police didn't stand a chance. Officer Bradley was one of the meanness asshole cops in the city. His entire squad was dirty. Marlo stood against a police car, wiping grass out of his head while Bradley cleaned his pockets and began passing his money out to the neighborhood residents. The police let everyone else go except for Marlo. He had the most cash back."

"You wanna sale drugs in the neighborhood? This is how you give Marlo concealed his anger and kept his focus on every single son of a bitch that put their greasy paws on his money. Across the street in Faye's bed room window, Eco peered out at his friend being restrained by law enforcement. He sent Faye out there to rescue him from a potential trespassing charge. After a few minutes, Eco breathed easy upon seeing Faye and Marlo walking back towards the apartment.

"Something told me not to go out there today," Eco remarked.

"Did you see all the money they took out that niggas pocket?" Kareem said surprisingly. "He gone be hot."

Weed smoke clouded the room as the stereo pumped, "**One love**" by Nas. Eco took a couple of pulls and passed the blunt. Before he could even blow the smoke out, Kareem was shoving another L in his face.

The door swung open and the beauty fiend walked in, frowning at the thick haze of smoke. Marlo trotted in behind her, taking a seat next to Eco.

"Let me hit that shit!" Everyone laughs, even Faye.

Eco passed the blunt, "damn nigga, you aight?"

"Hell nah!" Marlo said, taking a long pull off the weed. "Motherfuckers gave away some shit a my money!

I ain't even get a chance to count it. I remember their faces though and they gone give that bread back!"

"Fuck that shit cuz. You gonna make it back."

"I ain't trying to hear that shit. That was like $1500 they took off me!!! Thanks Faye, you saved my ass girl. They was about to give me a trespassing charge."

"Don't thank me nigga, just have my shit right by the time I come back upstairs."

"Damn, my nigga be home next week!" Eco chanted happily.

"Oh yeah, that's right, Jeffrey ass is coming home. It don't even seem like he been gone long," Kareem replied.

"Bet Tiffany sick as shit," Marlo adds.

"Cuz, I'm leaving soon as this chick pulls up. What y'all gonna do?" Asked Eco.

What y'all think nigga? People took all my paper, I'm about to beat the block up mane. I ain't going out until after 12, though. After the shift change. I ain't fucking with Bradley no more tonight."

Marlo stood ready to go upstairs, but paused at the startling sound of a annoying horn honking out front. He peeked out of the blinds.

"I think Belinda out there. Tell that hoe don't be blowing that loud ass horn, fuck she think she at."

Eco grabbed his pistol from the table and stuck it in his torso, totally ignoring Marlo's remark. "I'll see y'all niggas tomorrow."

The Ghost

CHAPTER 44

All Tiffany did was lay around, two ears filled with tears, leaving her pillow soaked. Waking up in this place seemed so unreal. Jeffrey was all she could think of. Two weeks had passed since she'd written him, and she prayed every night for a letter to come and replace her frown with a smile. Whenever she called to the streets, she'd ask about Jeffrey. Tiffany knew he was ready to come home, but didn't know the exact day.

Rakee paid her lawyer, then vanished off the face of the earth it seemed. He hadn't sent Tiffany one letter nor contacted Gloria to see how she was doing. Finally realizing that she was no more than a piece of meat to him, Tiffany thought back to her last conversation with Rakee. The sex had hypnotized her and it didn't matter if they were together or not. She was satisfied as long as she could get hers whenever she needed it.

Another month and Tiffany would be heading to court for sentencing. She and three friends sat at the round table playing spades. When the officer appeared at the gate with the mail bag, Tiffany didn't budge. All the females gathered around a huge table where the deputy emptied out the mail. As she called out names, girls took their letters and scurried off to their bunks to read them. Tiffany envied one pretty red bone. Every day, Tina had at least three letters coming in. She sat solemnly at the table waiting on her friends to return. At the sound of her name, Tiffany jumps up!

"Pass it!" She yells and quickly make her way over to the crowd.

A lesbian named Eva hesitates, smiling as she holds Tiffany's letter. "Who is Jeffrey?"

"Bitch, don't be looking at my mail!" Tiffany snatches the letter from her hand. "Need to mind your fucking business," she yells, storming off back to the table. Everyone in hearing distance was absolutely stunned to see the cute bashful chick lash out that way. Just the mention of Jeffrey's name, set off a fuse in her. Tiffany's heart pounded as she stared at the envelope. Changing her mind, she retreated over to her bed and hopped up on her bunk. She said a quick, silent prayer then opened the envelope.

Hey Tiff,

What's up girl? Nothing much here. By the time you get this scribe, I'll be home. Sorry for taking so long to write back, but I've been trying to take care of shit before I hit the streets. Anyways, I read your letter and believe it or not, I felt you. Tiffany, I don't hate you nor am I mad. These years I've been away have really helped me understand a lot of things. I'll separation only made me a stronger individual.

Shorty girl, I really loved you, and wanted so much to come home and be with you. Even though we haven't been on the best of terms, I'm sorry to hear about your predicament. I wouldn't wish this hell on my worst enemy. I don't even want to discuss why you are locked up, because I still find it hard to believe you went out like that.

Baby, all I wanted was for you to talk to me, but you treated me like a ghost, like I never existed in your world. And it CRUSHED ME....... But I'm good now. I read your letter over and over, feeling the pain behind your words. If we were to ever get back together, it wouldn't work out. I realized I could've treated you better out there, maybe told you I loved you more. But you didn't even give a nigga a chance to grow. When you left me, I vowed that the next girl I get with, will have all of me. I could never give you that Tiffany. Yeah everybody deserves a second chance but shorty, you stripped a nigga naked. I opened my heart up to you and you ripped it apart. I understand what you were going through out there and that's the only reason why I'm not mad. You threw our relationship on the crap table and lost. Now you have to accept your loss and keep going. Life goes on, right.

I'm here now, so if you need anything like money or whatever, just let your mama know and I will make sure you get it. Our relationship is over, but never will I leave a person I care about stranded when

they are down and out. I will always feel something in my heart for you. When you left, I knew it was real love from the way my heart felt. Some people live out their entire lives without ever experiencing true love. I feel blessed to have experienced it at a young age. And I thank God for the time we shared together.

While you are there, learn all that you can. Don't just waste time. It will be over before you know it, take care of yourself and don't forget to let Gloria know if you need something. Until next time, peace.....

Love is love Jeffrey

Tiffany folds the letter back up and gently places it back in the return envelope. She pulls the mattress back and put the letter under it, then balls herself up into a knotted fetal position and began to weep silently. Reality had slapped her in the face... And now she was scared, alone and stuck in this place.

CHAPTER 45

Jeffrey exhaled a sigh of relief as he walked out of the administration building of F. C. I. Lexington. The air even smelled different on the other side as he started down the long stretch of sidewalk, putting the horrible place behind him. The prison camp was directly across the street and campers looked on in envy, wishing it was them in Jeffrey's shoes. There were no words to describe the feeling of a prisoner officially being released. Goodbye to stand up count and trash talking C O's and the disgusting acts that occurred in prison, was now a thing of the past.

Wanda and Pernell yelled from the visitation parking lot the minute Jeffrey walked out. He felt like his old self again in his new, butter colored Timberland boots, blue Levy jeans and a matching Polo shirt. Wanda pulled out her camera and began to snap photos. After greeting everyone, Jeffrey turned for one last glimpse of the pitiful place, exhaled once more then proceeded to get inside the truck when out of nowhere, the door swung open!!! Jeffrey's eyes bulge with stunned excitement as Shonda steps out of the vehicle looking absolutely fabulous. Before he could muster a word, she happily jumps into his arms, landing the most passionate kiss dead on his lips.

"Alright now, you two have plenty of time for that," Wanda remarked with a smile. The little boy giggled at the lovebirds. Jeffrey had a private moment where he smiled inside at how everyone got together to surprise him by bringing Shonda along.

"I'm gonna get you Wanda," Jeffrey said and was all smiles. "You didn't tell me she was coming."

"Don't she looks cute, "Wanda teased. Jeffrey didn't respond right off, he simply observed the beauty standing before him. "Damn, I see you been taking real good care of yourself."

"I have..." Shonda blushes like a child under Jeffrey's watchful eye. "Boy, you just don't know how long I been waiting on this day."

"Is that right?"

Another hug and they all hops in the huge SUV. The ride back to Richmond was a long one. Wanda drove halfway and then gave the wheel to Shonda for the remainder of the ride. It was night time when they reached the city. Shonda had been planning this event for a while, reserving a room at the Marriott downtown for two days and taking time off from work.

Jeffrey had no objections of course. After two years of being locked up, a man longed for the day when he'd be able to lie next to a woman. For 48 hours, the couple laid up in the room having a ball. Shonda hadn't smoked or drank since Angie's death and Jeffrey had stopped as well. She had been fantasizing about getting with Jeffrey and now finally, here they were... Alone together and sexing one another morning, noon and night. Eco and the entire Avenue had been waiting on their man to show his face. Everyone kept hearing Jeffrey was home but no one had seen him. He called Prince the minute he got to the hotel. Jeffrey worked Shonda's body so well, that she didn't want to leave him. Driving up to Diane's house, Jeffrey's face flush with delight.

"Aye girl!!" Jeffrey hollers out the window at Britney. Before the car could stop good, Jeffrey was out and Britney rushed him. While he stood there showering the adorable little girl with hugs and kisses, Erica appeared in the doorway with her hands covering her mouth in pure shock.

He and Shonda made their way up to the porch, tears of joy leaping from Erica's eyes. She had her brother back, the first reunion since the death of their mother.

"Is that my baby?!" Diane yells excitedly from her upstairs bed room. She's downstairs in seconds.

"Yeah Mrs. Diane, it's me. I'm back in the world."

As Shonda got acquainted with Jeffrey's sisters, Jeffrey went to greet his best friend's mother with a hug and a kiss on her cheek. Diane stood a moment and observed Jeffrey with a smile as he entered the kitchen.

"What Mrs. Diane, why you looking at me that way?"

"Because I'm happy to see you. And you look good, don't he looks good y'all?"

"You got bigger I think," says Erica.

"Jeffrey, can you stay with us now? Please don't go back!" Britney whines. Jeffrey kneels down and kisses his baby sister, assuring her that he was there to stay "Okay then!" Britney says more than satisfied with his answer.

"You all have a seat, dinner is almost done. Excuse me, I need to run upstairs for a second."

Jeffrey turns to Erica the moment Diane leaves the room. "How long y'all been over here?"

"I think about six months," replies Erica.

"For real? But how-" he started to say when Diane returned. She sat across from Jeffrey and hands him a white envelope. Jeffrey eyes the envelope with a hint of curiosity. What was inside? As if its contents were sacred, Diane scrutinized Jeffrey before releasing a deep sigh.

"Jeffrey... I've been holding this for a long time now."

Jeffrey is totally dumbfounded. He opens the letter slowly. "I don't understand..."

"Read it Jeffrey." Diane urges him. Without further delay, he retrieves the letter and unfolds it.

The Ghost

Dear Mama,

How are you doing sweet heart? I thought long and hard before writing this letter. I just couldn't leave without talking to you. Thinking back, I can remember you asking me would you ever see me again. At the time, I didn't know how to tell you, but in my heart, I knew my time on this earth was running out.

I found the dude who killed Joanne and Angie, and I'm ready to see him for what he did. It's a good possibility I won't come out of this alive, but that's alright, mama because I rather die than rot in prison. I know I hurt you, but please understand that this life was just too much for me mama.

Don't go blaming yourself either because you did the best you could, a good job at that. No, it's not your fault! The game did this to me mama, the streets. Only thing I regret is not leaving you a grand baby. You know I'll always keep it real with you. Since I've been running, I did a lot of stuff I'm not proud of. You going to hear a lot of bad things about me after I'm gone.

I lost it out here mama. He stole my life from me when he killed Angie and I couldn't take no more.

I need you to do something for me because I can't rest until it's done. You know how I feel about Jeffrey. He's like the little brother I never had. I destroyed his life and everything he is going through is because of something I did. Joanne was all he had and it's my fault that she's gone, just like it's my fault that Angie is gone. Now can you see why I hurt so much? I am responsible for Jeffrey's sisters being taken away to. Get custody of them for me mama.... Please. After you do, I need you to get Britney and Erica a savings account, then split 75,000 between the three of them. Prince will clean the money for you and give you a check.

I love you mama. I know it's hard to lose your only son but in time you'll understand why I couldn't stay with you. I am not worried because I know you gonna take care of this for me, so I can sleep peacefully now. Take care of yourself for me lady and never forget that all wounds heal in time.

Love always Lamont

Although he blinked rapidly in an effort to disguise his emotions, a lonely tear trickled down Jeffrey's cheek.

"Where did this come from?"

"I was cleaning up one day and found it laying in the kitchen drawer, mixed up with the rest of the bills. One of the kids must have gotten it out of the mailbox and didn't tell me. It's been sitting there since he died but I didn't find it until seven months later."

"You got custody of them?"

"I sure do. Right after I found that letter, I called Wanda and told her I would do it. She took me to see....

What's her name baby?"

"Mrs. Anderson." Erica reply.

"That's her, Mrs. Anderson. She's really nice to. We didn't even set a court date. She took me straight in front of the Judge and he granted me custody on the spot. They've been here ever since."

Jeffrey immediately raise to a stance, rounds the table and gives Mrs. Diane an enormous hug. "THANK YOU."

"You are welcome honey. They are my babies, I told them I wanted to surprise you."

"And surprise you did," Jeffrey said looking up at Erica. "The best surprise I could get!" He stare at the letter, still amazed that LA had written it. "Damn my nigga...."

"So how does it feel to be home?" Diane asked. He looked at everyone in the room.

"It feels like heaven Mrs. Diane, I swear! This must be what heaven feels like." He tears up when he says this. Shonda leans over to kiss Jeffrey as he wraps her in his arms.

"Diane, when the food gone be ready, because somebody done took all my energy away!" Shonda nudge him then blushes as everyone erupts in laughter.

"I know that's right. What's your mama doing girl? Diane ask.

"Oh nothing, she working hard, "Shonda replied.

"Tell her I asked about her."

"Alright."

"Come on Erica, help me fix these plates. Everyone heads to the kitchen.

"Damn, that smells good," Shonda says, entranced by the fragrant aroma coming from the oven. After the plates were fixed, everyone gathered around the table. As Britney proceeded with the grace, Jeffery's mind flashed back to the morning of their mothers shooting. The whole family had sat down to eat breakfast just like now. He looked around at everyone and couldn't believe that he was actually home.

"Thank God." He closes the blessing, then commenced his ravenous attack on the delicious meal.

CHAPTER 46

The family had returned to their Chesterfield home to await Jeffery's arrival. Prince and Pernell were tossing around a football in the backyard when Wanda escorted Jeffrey and Shonda through the side gate. Although Jeffrey did his best at masking his disappointment over Prince's current physical condition, the O G could easily see past the smile. Hearing about it and seeing it in person, was two entirely different things. Prince was like superman to the city's youth and in Jeffrey's eyes, he'd always been a giant. But to arrive and see the mighty fucking O G in a wheel chair, Jeffrey just couldn't have prepared himself for it.

"Lil man, we gonna play later alright?" Prince tells his son when Jeffrey arrives.

"Okay daddy," the kid bellows out before taking off towards his mother.

"Damn bro, what's good?" Prince says smiling from ear to ear as he rolls over to Jeffrey and extends out his hand.

"Prince... My nigga.... Mane, what it do." Jeffrey utters as he kneels to give Prince a heartfelt hug. It's an emotional reunion as they embrace, both of them fighting not to shed a tear in front of each other.

"Awww, look at them," Wanda says teasingly as she walks up with Shonda.

Who is this? I don't believe we've met." Prince refers to Shonda who comes to stand next to Jeffrey, blushing terribly. Wanda smiles inside at the way people reacted to her man.

"I'm Shonda. Nice to meet you." They shake hands.

"You look familiar," Prince remarks .

"This is Angie's sister," Jeffrey replies.

"You serious?" Prince says excitedly, then looks closely at Shonda. "Sorry to hear about Angie. She was a real nice girl."
"Thanks."

Jeffrey pulls her into his arms, noticing the subject made her a little up tight.

"No wonder she looked familiar," Prince commented.

Jeffrey takes in the lavish set up Prince has and states, "mane I'm fucking with this spot. This how a nigga suppose to live."

Prince found himself gazing at the beautiful view, "yeah man, I had this place for about three years. Real peaceful out here. This ain't shit, check out the inside. Give them a quick tour of the crib baby."

"Word." Jeffrey reaches for Shonda's hand, waiting for Wanda to lead the way. After kissing Prince gently on the neck, Wanda and her guest enters through the back patio with Pernell following close behind. Prince let go of a big sigh.

It had definitely been a long journey for the kid. Thoughts of Jeffrey always stayed on his mind, hoping he was learning something in prison, rather than sitting back simply doing time. Did he change any? Was he ready to tackle the world and live out his dreams? Prince was glad to have him back, but first he needed to get inside his mind to see where his head was. Prince wipes his moist eyes when he hears them return. Wanda had given Jeffrey and his girl friend a quick tour of their spacious home. Jeffrey came back hyped, "yo bro, you got this place laid man! It don't even look that big from out here."

"You like it?" Asked Prince.

"Hell yeah!"

Wanda, Shonda and Pernell had just exited the house when Jeffrey was pushing Prince to the front yard.

"We gone be in the garage talking baby," Prince hollers over his shoulder.

As they approach the two car garage, Prince hit a button on his key chain. The electric door opens, revealing a shiny black Mercedes with factory wheels. Beside it was a new fully equipped, royal blue Honda Accord EX.

"Damn Prince, how many whips do you have?" Jeffrey walked circles around the cars in astonishment.

"Brand new and neither one got over a thousand miles."

The youngster leaned on the Mercedes and turned to face the O G.

"Aye Prince, its fucked up what happen to you."

"You didn't expect this huh. Me in this chair."

"Hell no! I mean, I heard that you was paralyzed and all. But damn! You good, though?"

"Of course. I take a licking and keep on ticking," Prince jokes, trying to make light of his predicament.

"When I first got hit and learned I would never walk again, I was mad at the world. But life is like that.

One thing that I've learned in this life is, it don't give a shit about you. It don't stop just because you hurting or going through rough times.

With or without you, the world keeps turning." Prince looked up at Jeffrey and they shared a mutual gaze. "I've accepted this shit, you know. Got caught slipping."

"I'm just glad you made it through that."

"Yeah, so how you doing? Where you at mentally?"

The youngster flushed with excitement. "You know I was building with the Islam Nation. I met a good friend in prison. The brother taught me so much. His name is Kihiem, head Minister at Lexington." Jeffrey went into deep thinking about his prison mentor.

"He changed my life Prince. I swear mane. I was about to self destruct, especially when I called home and heard what happened to you."

"Sounds like you got your mind right. So what you plan on doing now?"

"I've been writing my whole bid, and my shit tight. I had the whole prison feeling me. I was hoping you could put me down. You said that when shit blew over, you'd do what you could to help me."

Stroking the thick hair on his goatee, Prince responds. "I did say that, didn't I? How old is Erica, can she drive yet?"

"She just 15, why you ask? What's up?"

"How you think she'll look behind the wheel of this pretty bitch?" Prince asks. "Ain't but a couple people got it." Prince let his hand glide across the clean Mercedes hood.

"Hold up! You gonna let my little sister push your brand new ride?"

"Hell no! I'll leave that up to the owner." Prince tosses Jeffrey a brand new set of keys. "That is............... If he can part with it for that long!!!!!!" Jeffrey walks around the car. "You for real?"

"I brought both of them last month. The Honda for Erica. Now all you gotta do is get a license."

"I don't know what to say."

"Jeffrey you can't be parking expensive cars like this in the hood." Jeffrey agreed.

"You say you like the house right?"

The expression on Jeffrey's face is priceless. "Are you fucking kidding me?" Do I like the house??!!" Jeffrey's eyes darted around the lavishly decorated room as he turned back to Prince. "I love this fucking house!!!"

"Think it's big enough for you and your sisters?"

"Big enough?" He repeats. "Are you being serious right now mane?"

"I want you to have it for you and your family."

"What do you mean, have it? I gotta pay rent?"

"The house is yours. I signed the deed over to you and Erica. Its paid for. You pay the mortgage of course."

"**WHAT!!!! Prince!!!!** You gotta be shitting me mane."

"It's just your time man," Prince says smoothly. "A lot of cats couldn't walk in your shoes Jeff. Been through hell and back and you still standing tall. You deserve all this shit and more."

"Prince, I don't understand, why me mane?"

"Why not you?"

"You been looking out for me all these years."

"Remember when your mom was first shot? And I told you everything in life had a reason behind it."

"I remember like it was yesterday."

"I can't get into it right now but there is a reason." Prince reaches in his jacket pocket and pulls out a piece of paper. "I'll be here at 2:00 tomorrow. Make sure you come, we got a lot to talk about."

Jeffrey stares at the paper. "I'll be there. What time you got?" Prince glances at his Tag Huer, "3:30."

"I gotta meet Eco up at the mall." Jeffrey got behind the wheel chair and pushed Prince through the doorway. As they left the garage, the youngster paused.

"Prince, let me get this straight. You mean to tell me you giving me a house and two brand new cars?"

Prince looks up, "you want me to pinch you so you know you ain't dreaming?"

"Alright cool, just had to make sure I heard you right.

CHAPTER 47

Half the city patronized Springfield Mall. Throughout the week, various big time hustlers could be spotted in the clothing stores spending thousands of dollars. Some cats just came to see the ladies. Store owners knew exactly what they were doing by hiring attractive young female employees.

Sea Dreams Leathers had the prettiest saleswomen and they had game too. One flash of that cute smile and out came bankrolls, along with the game spitting. Small time hustlers got little play. The girls knew exactly who the hood legends were when a real playa entered the store. Everything stopped. Whenever Rakee showed his face, girls knew what time it was. He was a big spender, and never shopped just for himself. His long braids hung pass his shoulders as he crouched down to try on some new Polo boots he'd ordered out of the stores catalog weeks before. On the counter, he had well over a few thousand bucks worth of merchandise, mostly clothes for his son and his daughter.

"Rakee, how old is your daughter?" Tasha, the sexy sales clerk asks.

He stands up with one boot on, looking down to see how it looked on his foot. "She be four this year. Go ahead and ring these up too. Shorty, I know you can find a button up shirt or something to match."

She grabs the other boot out of the box. "I saw something earlier that would go perfect with these. Give me a couple of minutes and I'll be right back."

Rakee took a seat and slipped his Jordan's back on his feet. As he sat on the bench, tying up one of his shoe laces, he glanced up in time to see a couple of Tiffany's loud mouth friends enter the store. He mouthed a quiet,

"Goddamn."

Trina had entered the store with two of Tiffany's friends who walked up and stopped by him.

"Hi Rakee, you ain't gotta act like that. You can speak nigga." She stood over him with one hand on her hip.

"What's good Trina, how you doing? Hey y'all," Rakee says and squeezes out a tight smile, noticing everyone had spoken except for Ayesha. She rolled her eyes at Rakee.

"What's up shorty, you got something on your mind?"

"As a matter a fact I do. For starters, why you do my girl like that?" When Trina tried to hush her, she ignored her. "No girl, because that shit won't right!"

"Hold up, Trina," Rakee replies with a hint of anger in his tone. "Ayesha, who the fuck is you? All y'all bitches was wrong for what y'all did!" Rakee hesitates his next statement when he sees people in the store taking notice.

"Give me a minute," Rakee says and gestures to Tasha who was now standing at the counter with his clothes. He quickly focused his attention back on the girls.

"Tiffany know why I don't fuck with her. Shorty girl was out of line and she knew where we stood. That crazy bitch stabbed my daughter's mother. I don't owe you a damn thing."

Ayesha was so furious, her eyes burned with tears. "Don't worry about that nigga," her sister Tanya says patting her shoulder for comfort.

"For real though, Tiffany's ass was wrong. She should never have cut that girl," Trina finally admits. "Fuck that shit, I'm hungry. Let's go to the food court."

Tanya lead the way toward the front of the store. As they approached the exit, Rakee was leaning over the counter with a knot of cash.

"Bye Rakee. We still cool right?" Trina asked him on their way out.

"Fasho, we good. Ya'll take care."

Trina and Ayesha bumps into Jeffrey and Eco as they were leaving the store. They all holler his name simultaneously. And Trina sees Shonda by his side and immediately starts poking.

"Shonda, what are you doing here?"

"I'm with Jeffrey." Shonda admits and smiles inside as they stare her down.

"Humph," Trina gestures.

"Hey Eco and Marlo," Ayesha greets.

Trina happen to glance back and see Jeffrey and Eco whispering about something. She wondered what about. But then her curiosity was silenced and she was able to put it together when Rakee stepped foot out of **Sea Dreams Leathers** with both hands filled with shopping bags. At that point, everything seemed to slow up. Marlo and Eco ice grilled Rakee as he walked pass. Shonda even felt the negative energy, although she was clueless as to what was happening around her.

Rakee took one look at the new face with the fresh prison glow and knew instantly that he was standing face-to-face with Jeffrey. Plus, he remembered his face from a portrait in Tiffany's bedroom. They shared an awkward moment. This cat was the cause of a lot of Jeffery's anguish while in prison.

Rakee didn't know what to expect from Jeffrey. He didn't want any drama, so he proceeded on his way. Jeffrey grabbed Shonda by the hand and lead her into the store, whispered something to his boys before exiting back out the store.

Rakee had reached Radio Shack, which was two stores down when he turned and recognized Jeffrey walking behind him alone. Immediately upon approach, Rakee let his bags fall to the ground so that his hands would be free. He had heard about Jeffrey and his crew. That he hung around killers and that his hood had been responsible for the rise in the murder rate in recent years.

'What the fuck could he possibly want?' Rakee wondered.

Sensing his uneasiness, Jeffrey quickly said, "cuz... It ain't even that type a visit. I ain't got no beef with you homey. I just wanna rap to you on some real nigga shit."

Rakee was relieved. "Okay cool, we can slide right over there then." Rakee points to a bench directly across from a quiet photo shop.

"Yo Jeffrey... I'm glad you called me because it's something I wanna say to you." They were face-to-face now. "First, I'm glad to see you home. Second, I want you to know that I never once disrespected you. I been down before so I know how it goes. Third man, if I caused you any type of pain, I apologize."

Jeffrey let him speak freely without interrupting. And when he was done, Jeffrey hesitated, trying to choose his words carefully. "You know, I don't blame you for Tiffany leaving me. If you could come along and take her away like that, then homey, she was never mine from the start. Honestly, I called you to let you know that we don't got any problems. What shorty did is dead. I'm home now so when we cross paths, it's cool to speak. She paying for what she did now. Oh and I know you and my boys done had a few run ins." Jeffrey extends out his hand in good faith and they shake.

"We gone peace this shit out right now because it's too many females out here to beef over one."

"No doubt my nigga," Rakee replied giving Jeffrey dap. "Cuz I like yo style and I'm glad we got a chance to talk."

When they were done talking, the two guys walks off in opposite directions. On his way back to Sea Dreams Leathers, Jeffrey stops in his tracks and focuses his attention on three women and a small child standing near Chicken Filet inside the food court. Jeffrey strained his eyes at the female holding the child. She looked familiar. He returned to the store where he left Shonda. She had a few items on the counter for him to buy and Eco had purchased a leather coat that matched his boots.

"You like these joints right here Jeffrey." Asked Marlo as he pointed to a variety of fresh new leathers hanging on the wall.

"Yeah, the black and gray is like that. Let me see that in a 3X." Tasha had definitely struck gold today. Just about everyone who had come to the store in the past hour, called on her. She quickly grabbed the pole used to unhook the coats and pulled Jeffrey's coat from the wall. Shonda walked over. "I gotta get to work. You alright with Eco?"

"Yeah I can get Eco to drop me off. Did you see anything you wanted in here?"

"Well I did see a coat I thought was cute. But it cost too much?"

"What do it cost?"
Shonda flashed a timid smile and mumbled, "$400."

"Oh shit!! You right.. That is too much."

Shonda slightly frowns.

"I'm only joking," Jeffrey teased. "You want it?"

"Hell yeah I want it!!!"

After taking the coat to the sales lady at the counter, Shonda gave Jeffrey a big juicy kiss and thanked him for the gift, then rushed off to work. Jeffrey had bumped into a number of people he hadn't seen in years. Girls from school saw Jeffrey and went berserk. He was glad Shonda had left because the chicks were sweating him in a major way.

After leaving another shoe store, Jeffrey and his friends started toward the food court. "Look at Keisha over there!" Eco says. "But she with that sucka though."

"Shorty looking right too," Jeffrey observed. Keisha stood in front of Victoria Secrets talking to some lame she'd been seeing for a couple of months now. The guy noticed the change in her expression when Jeffrey walked by. Her guy turned instantly to catch a glimpse of what had captured her attention.

"Aye y'all," Keisha spoke, her eyes beaming on Jeffrey in a suggestive manner. He simply grinned.

"Holla at you boy," he yelled back, causing his friends to double over in laughter. Seconds later, he peeped over his shoulder and saw that the couple appeared to be engaging in a heated argument. Approaching the huge eatery, Jeffrey's main concern was finding a seat. He told Eco to order him a couple slices of cheese pizza, then headed over to the nearest empty table and sat. His first day back in the world, he couldn't sit still from reckless eye balling the cute females that strolled by.

"Damn it feels good to be home." As he continued to admire the scenery, he suddenly noticed the same group of women he saw earlier. They were sitting about 50 yards to the left of him.

"There she goes again," Jeffrey utters to no one in particular. It was that girl again. There was something strikingly familiar about her that kept his eyes fixated on her. For one, she was gorgeous and her body was right. She looked in Jeffrey's direction and caught him staring. Embarrassed, he got up to find Eco and check on their pizza. The food was ready and the three grabbed slices and returned to their seats. As they began to chow down, Jeffrey turned slightly in his chair to look for the girl again, only to find her now gawking in his direction!!

Eco notices her and says, "Ol girl over there eye balling one of us.

You know her J?"

By the time Jeffrey turned around, the woman was now pointing in their direction. "Damn nigga, you done came up!" Marlo raved.

Jeffrey flashed a perfect set of pearl whites. "It must be the glow," he said and stood to his feet, a bit confused by the girls giant smile. He was halfway to her when he came to a complete stop.

"Oh hell no..... It can't be!!!" He mutters under his breath. It's only when he was close up on her, did he finally recognize her. They scream each other's name simultaneously.

"Dana!!! I can't fucking believe it!!!"

"Jeffrey!!! Oh my God boy, where have you been???"

"I was looking at you earlier and ain't know who the hell you was. I can't believe this shit, what's been up?"

"I knew it was you boy! Do you know how long I've been looking for you? I have moved down here and everything. Where you been?"

Before Jeffrey could respond, he glanced down at the cute kid clinging to her leg. "What's up lil man?" He held out his hand as the handsome toddler slapped it and giggled. "Dana I got arrested a couple weeks after we split. I just came home three days ago."

A look of horror suddenly falls over her face.

"No... It wasn't for that. They got me on a gun charge. Who is this lil guy?" Jeffrey nods down at the kid.

Smiling pleasantly, Dana kisses the child's forehead. "This is my son Jeffrey."

Jeffrey never knew Dana to have any kids so when she mentioned the boy being her son, his shock was more than obvious. The child looked at his mother then across at the stranger. Jeffrey's palms immediately becomes clammy as he searches Dana's eyes for answers. She ask Jeffrey to have a seat. As both of them sat, Dana briefly introduces Jeffrey to her cousin and aunt.

"Thee Jeffrey?" Her cousin Boo Boo blurts out. As they prepare to take the boy to give the long lost friends some privacy, Jeffrey looks over his shoulder to check on his boys and smiles at Eco signaling for him to put him down with Dana's cousin.

"We gone take baby LA for a stroll while you two talk. Come on baby," aunt Cheryl says before picking up the toddler. "Well, nice meeting you Jeffrey."

"Bye Jeffreyyy!" Boo Boo says in a flirtatious tone.

Shaking her head, Dana says, "I think my cousin likes you."

Returning to their conversation, he eyes Dana seriously. "You named him after LA. That was cool. You really loved that nigga, didn't you?"

"He's L A's son Jeffrey."

"How did I know you would say that."

"I don't know if you and him ever talked about me, or if he told you how we met... But it was wild. LA was the only man I ever had unprotected sex with. We was together three weeks. Can you believe I fell in love with a man who kidnapped me?"

"Hold up right quick." Jeffrey's friends were approaching their table.

"Aye cuz, we gone walk to Macy's real quick," says Eco. They leave their bags with Jeffrey and walks off.
"When I first found out I was pregnant, it ain't come as a surprise

and I knew exactly who's baby it was. Anyway, I made an appointment to get an abortion. I couldn't afford to have a baby with no father and my family was totally against it. Plus, I wanted to go to college. I woke up early that morning, ready to just get it over with." Dana stares off into space. "I sat in the waiting room and all I could seem to think about was him... LA. He killed a man right in front of me then put the gun to my head and told me to get behind the wheel and drive!! Shit, I did it because I didn't wanna die."

Jeffrey could see the toll that speaking about their past was having on her.

"Then he cried like a baby in front of me right after shooting someone. When he finally got around to telling me about Angie, I felt so bad for him, that he had me in tears. He was going to prison for life if he got caught. He even listened on the phone while Angie was being raped and killed. All he used to talk about to me was the baby she lost."

"Now I understand why he ain't wanna live no more. I thought about all that while I was sitting there, waiting to have our baby aborted. I couldn't do it. LA changed my life Jeffrey for the better. I moved down here to look for you, so that you could take me to his mother. When I couldn't find you, I was ready to start asking people because I knew somebody knew y'all, but I was scared. These niggas are heartless out here. I didn't want nothing to happen to me or my baby, just look at what happen to Angie. I didn't know nobody down here but my family so I just kept hoping that I would run into you... I even went past the old apartment building I dropped you off at that night."

Jeffrey was absolutely stunned. "Damn shorty, I'm jive fucked up for real! So you telling me my nigga got a son."

"All you have to do is look at him. I don't even have a picture of LA, but I know my son looks just like him. Do the math, his first birthday was two months ago." A smile appears on Dana's face as she looks up to see her aunt and cousin on their way back with her son.

"They're coming now, look at him and tell me what you think." Jeffrey turns around in his chair and watches the boy as they move at a slow gait. His heart starts beating fast and his palms began to sweat.

"Come to mama," Dana says and gently takes hold of the boy. The child grins at Jeffrey and in that same instant, his heart does somersaults. His best friends features were all over this boy. From L A's smile, to that one distinctive dimple on his chunky cheek, he was definitely his father's son.

"I gotta call Diane."

"Is that his mother? How do you think she'll take it?"

"I don't know. But it ain't no way she can deny him." The child was now facing Jeffrey and smiling from ear to ear.

"This little guy is the spitting image of the baby pictures she got on her wall." Jeffrey laughs. "I gotta call and prepare her for this shit. She might fuck around and have a asthma attack!"

"Stop playing," Dana hit him playfully as they both share a great laugh.

"Are you for real?" Boo Boo ask.

"Hell yeah!! A baby that looks just like that nigga!! This is gone mess her up. In a good way though."

CHAPTER 48

It was one 1:50 p.m. when Prince glanced at his watch before turning off his computer. Backing up in his wheelchair, he does a 360 in the middle of the floor. It didn't take long for him to get accustomed to using the wheelchair, popping willies and showing off at times for Pernell. He didn't want his son or anybody for that matter treating him differently because of his condition. And though Wanda pampered him at times, she knew where to draw the line. He was still very active and would shun any-one who showed him sympathy.

Prince rolled himself over to where Wanda and his son were lounging, parking his two wheels in front of the long leather sofa. The boy jumped up and ran to his father. "Dad, who named you Prince? Mama won't tell me, she said to ask you."

Wanda sat back waiting anxiously, curious herself as to how her man received such a name. Prince pondered over the question for a mo-ment.

"If I can remember correctly, it was your grandma who used to rock me in her arms when I was a baby and call me her little Prince. My uncle Butch put the nick name out there and it stuck."

"So dad, is Butch my uncle too?"

"Yup, he's your great uncle."

Wanda sauntered over next to the love of her life, hovered over him and kissed him gently. Your daddy ain't no prince." She massages his neck.

"He's a KING!" She kissed her man ever so gently on the cheek.

"Ya'll cut that out!!!" Jeffrey remarks humorously as he makes a surprise visit.

"Jeffrey?"

"Young blood!" Prince exclaimed, stopping in the middle of the floor. Monitors surrounded the entire studio. In the very back, was a master mixing room. Every wall was sound proof, and black carpet covered the whole floor. The engineer had constant view of all booths from his spot in the mixing room.

Jeffrey was beyond impressed by the immaculate layout. "Hey there Wanda.... What up Pernell?!" He held his hand out for the kid, "you getting tall too boy. Aye, I rode past this building twice."

"Come on Pernell, we going to get something to eat. Jeffrey, how you get here?" Wanda asked.

"Shonda drop me off before she went to work. I had to go to DMV this morning." He flashes his Learners Permit proudly, adding that the official L's would come in the mail.

"Gotta test out my new ride."

"Bye baby," Wanda says kissing Prince goodbye. Pernell was on her heels as they all left out the door.

Jeffrey wandered off to the booth. "You too good to me mane!"

"Just take care of the place Jeff. How long they got you on papers?"

"Three years. If I do good, I'll be off in two."

"Well, you got your work cut out for you. When you gonna lay some of that shit on a track? You keep saying you tight. Shit, I'm ready to hear something!" Prince was eager.

"You got your own studio, what you gonna do?" Jeffrey was fixing to reply to Prince when his last statement registered in Jeffrey's mind.

"Huh?" Jeffrey snaps out of his trance. "My bad Prince, it's just. Why.............. You too good to me mane! I ain't no ungrateful nigga, but this is a lot Unc."

"Come over here. Take a seat Jeffrey. It's time we talk about this." Jeffrey walked over and plopped down on a plush, white leather couch, facing the incapacitated O G.

"I'm sure you've heard all about my crew back in the day, right?" The youngster nods in conformation. "I knew your daddy. You remind me of him. Your father was one of the true ones."

"You knew him?" Jeffrey was ecstatic. Prince had never mention his father to him before, so he was anxious to know more.

"What do you remember about him?"

"Mane, I remember back when I was like ten years old. We was tight too. Every morning dad would walk me to the bus stop. We would wake up early to mama cussing him out for being on the streets all night. No matter how late he came in or if he came in at all, he was always there in the morning to walk me to the bus stop." His voice trails off.....

"I remember his funeral like it was yesterday. I went the fuck off, beating on the casket and shit, almost knocking it off the stand. It was wild Prince. I had this poem I wrote for him. Yeah......... This poem for the funeral. I stood there reading it and got mad as hell because I wanted to talk to my daddy, but he wasn't there. He was gone mane and no matter how loud I yelled the words at the casket, he wasn't reacting. Wasn't gonna open his mouth to tell me how much he liked it."

Jeffrey seemed to relive the moment as he vividly recalled the tragic event to Prince with a blank eyed stare. There was a long silence as the youngster resumed his recollection, "how I will miss you ....

words cannot describe the love you showed our family while you were here," he recited the poem. "Although, at times I've been wrong-"

"You remained patient, guiding me out of the darkness, and making me strong," Prince interjects, finishing the line to Jeffrey's creation.

The youngster jumps off the couch, gawking at his mentor as if he'd seen a ghost, "how? How did you know-"

"I was there Jeffrey... Your father, he went just as hard as us, a true soldier. My right-hand man Justice." Prince pauses, fidgeting nervously with his hands.

"Well back then we was making niggas pay dues and what not. We was taking shit and those who refused, we stuck it to them hard. One day Justice pulled up on your pops and his boys with a few niggas from the crew.

They pressed everyone for dough, but your dad ain't budge, held his ground... Jeffrey... In the end, your old man paid with his life, but went to his grave with honor and much respect."

"What I'm telling you is......... My best friend killed your father."

It took a moment for Prince's words to sink in before Jeffrey responded.

"Why you telling me this now? Is that why you been looking out for me? Cause your man killed my dad?"

Prince nods slowly. "There's more to it than that though, Jeffrey. Do you believe in forgiveness?"

"It depends."

"On what?" Prince asked

"The situation. Where you going with this Prince?"

"Could you ever forgive the man for what he did to your father?"

"Prince, that's your man, I don't even know dude. On top of that, he killed my dad mane. How I look forgiving this cat? So where your partner at now? I don't know what you want me to say."

The O G chose his words carefully. "Jeffrey, in life everything is not always what it seems. Situations that seem simple can quickly become complicated, leaving you to make difficult decisions." Prince sighs. "Man, fuck this shit!!! Kihiem is Justice. Kihiem killed your father."

Time stood still for the youngster as Prince's devastating confession echoed through his head. Overtaken by the words as they registered in his brain, Jeffrey's body went limp on the sofa. He stayed in that position for a few moments, then came to face the grim reality as he sprung from the chair.

"You gotta be fucking kidding me!!! Prince, not Kihiem! Anybody but Kihiem!"

"I know how you feel Jeffrey. Believe me, that shit was killing me inside."

Jeffrey did not say a word, just slouched back in his chair as if he'd just been smacked by a Mac Truck. Right there he began to reflect back on his time in prison and the brief time he and Kihiem spent together. He finally understood why the Islam Nation always came to his aid. The third day he was there, the Muslims brought over a big bag of canteen, jogging suit and a fresh pair of sneakers. Then there was the fight with the Gd's. If it weren't for the brothers, the gang would've demolished Jeffrey out there.

"Damn, so that's why you never came to see me huh. You ain't want the Feds to think you was communicating back with the Juice Crew?"

"Yup," Prince replied. "You seen it for yourself how bad they got it out for me."

"Oh shit," Jeffrey says and jumps up. "Now that I'm thinking about it, Kihiem... He was trying to tell me!!"

"What you mean?"

"About three weeks before I got released, we was out on the yard. We had just finished working out. Now that I remember, Kihiem was act-ing strange as hell. He told me that we needed to talk. He was about to say something when they announced recall. But I remember... He was real sad that night. First time I ever saw him like that... Damn, Kihiem killed my dad."

"I know that it's hard for you, but you still have to be smart about this. Let me explain something about Justice and all of us. Back in the 80s, we ran the streets like mad men. You know how it is. Lots of people died, good people like your father. Justice is a different man now. I ain't seen him in over 10 years, but I know he regrets killing your pops. You think it was easy for him to look you in the eyes knowing the circumstances?"

"I remember coming home from prison and seeing you out there and I felt terrible inside." Prince smiles and shakes his head. "Your mother though, she was tough and a proud woman. I always wanted to help her but she would never accept it from me. I know what it feels like growing up without a father, but what matters Jeffrey is that we both made it. You gotta look at the big picture then make a decision. Remember the condi-tion you was in before you met Kihiem or Justice? Yes, he killed your old man and probably was the reason why your life has been so fucked up. He knows this. Why do you think he worked so hard to get you right mental-ly? Teaching and building with you was the only opportunity he had to give back. If it wasn't for Justice, I wouldn't be where I am today."

Jeffrey listened intensely. He didn't know what to say, so he said nothing. Just when he thought his life couldn't get any more complicated, this happens. This was the wildest shit that could ever happen. But he re-called the killing like it was yesterday. Jeffrey witness the execution through a crack in his bedroom window. The deafening gun shots and his father falling to the ground, a tow of Cadillac's speeding off from the scene. His mothers piercing cry is what stuck out the most though. It's what snapped him back from staring at the bloody remnants of his father bleeding on the cold pavement. He contemplated murder at a very young age. At just ten years old, he told his mom that he wanted to grow up fast so that he could find his father's killer. But he didn't have to wonder or go looking for him anymore. ***His fathers killer had found him...***

"It's all on you whether or not you decide to forgive him. Just remember, he gave you knowledge of self. True, he took life from your father but he also gave you back yours."

The youngsters mind was clouded with mixed emotions. He chuckled, trying to conceal his hurt as he faced at his mentor.

"I feel everything that you say Prince, but this shit jive got me stuck! I still love this dude though... How the fuck can I love this nigga now under the circumstances?" Jeffrey sat down. "Mane, I don't even know what to say right now for real."

"There's no rush, just take your time. I'm confident that you'll make the right choice." Prince let his words marinate in Jeffrey then he moves on to other business. "I can't believe this shit you telling me about LA having a son"

"Oh yeah, that's his kid alright for the world. My nigga spit him out.

"Yeah man, I can't wait to see him. You told his mama yet?"

"I did and she is excited."

"So Jeffrey, are we still cool? I mean you ain't mad at me are you??"

"Never Prince, never that. I understand why you couldn't tell me. Now in my adolescent stages, I probably would've been heated, but I'm good. I got to keep my head clear."

"I like the sound of that. So, are you still going to be my best man?"

"Get out of here, are you serious?" The youngster drops down on the couch in an emotional outburst.

"We've been through a lot and I figured it's about time we make this thing official. Just need you to be there with me."

"Say no more, I'm there! So when is it gone happen?"

"Sometime next month. It's gonna be kind of private though, just the family and close friends. Jeff, I'm about to take a break from the city for a while. I got a spot down in Atlanta, it's a nice place man. You need to come out and visit sometimes. I'm tired of Richmond. I feel like I can kick back and rest now that you straight. So how do you feel?"

Jeffrey reveals a wide grin. "*On top of the world Prince.......... On top of the world!*"

CHAPTER 49

Diane stayed awake all night after hanging up with Jeffrey. L A's baby pictures in hand, she stepped over to peer out of the window but there was still no sign of them. She couldn't wait to see this baby. Although Jeffrey swore that the child looked like her son, she had mixed feelings. Who was this girl and why would she wait two years later? Diane knew how deceptive women could be, especially when money was involved.

An angry grimace fail over her face as she thought of someone trying to play games with her emotions. Diane pictured her son on the run, all the things she'd seen in the papers and on the news, yet and still, she couldn't bring herself to believe that her son had done the things he was accused of.

"It's no way he had time to be out there making babies," she mumbled bitterly.

Diane was standing in her screen door when a Mercedes pulled up into her driveway. 'Who is that?' Then she recognized Jeffrey behind the wheel.

"Boy who's pretty car have you stolen? You ain't out here doing wrong already, are you?"

Jeffrey laughed hard at her comment. "No Mrs. Diane, this is my car. You know I ain't going out like that. It was a gift from Prince." He greeted her with his usual hug and kiss on the cheek. "Erica and Britney in school huh?"

"Yeah, my babies gone. It be so lonely in here when they leave."

Diane appears to drift off for a moment in thought. She snaps back. "So what's the deal with this girl Jeffrey? It better not be no funny shit." Diane had Jeffrey in tears from laughing. They sat for a while shooting the breeze.

"Where the hell is she? I am anxious to see this child!"

Jeffrey sat up straight. "Diane I'm telling you," he started to say when a burgundy Mazda 626 drives up and parks directly behind Jeffrey's Benz.

"I'll just let you see for yourself," Jeffrey says and hops off the porch to meet Dana.

"What's up y'all?" He peeks his head in the backseat at Boo Boo's fine ass. "Aye Boo Boo, what's good?"

"Hi Jeffrey." She blushed terribly. Baby LA was sitting in his baby seat, wide awake and looking handsome in his baby blue Polo jumpsuit and matching Jordan's. Dana carefully removed the toddler from his seat then straightened the Polo cap on his head.

Diane paced about on her porch like an inpatient kid. Her heart pounded as Jeffrey introduced everyone. As Dana extended out her hand for the older woman to shake, Diane had fallen into a trance at the mere sight of her potential grand baby. "Look at you!" She coos, ignoring everybody else. She totally disregards Dana's extended hand to get to the child. Immediately, tears comes to surface.

"I don't believe it," Diane gasp as she opens her arms and receives the small boy and hold him up. "I mean... He looks just like my son!!" The child displays nothing but gums, obviously comfortable with the stranger. Without another word, Diane turns on her heels and heads up to the porch, leaving Jeffrey and Dana in the middle of the sidewalk.

Over her shoulder, she yells, "ya'll can come on in and tell who ever that is in the car to come on in."

When the four walked in the room, Diane was sitting on the couch talking baby jibber to LA Jr. Photo albums were spread across the dining room table.

"Have a seat and make yourselves comfortable." Dana was admiring baby pictures of LA. She looked over at her son and back at the photos. "He looks just like him. Oh my God, I gotta have a copy of these." Jeffrey hands her another picture album with more recent photos. Diane was lost in her own world, playing with her grandson. This was a very special moment and Diane had already made up her mind that her only grandson would be spoiled rotten. Jeffrey flirted with Boo Boo, complementing her lovely smile and enjoying her involuntary blush as they conversed.

Dana's aunt Cheryl suddenly looked around the living room curiously and became concerned when she didn't see Dana.

"Did you see where Dana went?" Boo Boo shrugs her shoulders and continues her talk with Jeffrey. Cheryl goes to look for her. She was headed toward the downstairs bathroom when her ears caught peculiar sounds. As she got closer, the noises became louder. Cheryl called her name and got no reply. Then she saw Dana sitting on the steps alone and staring at a photo of LA.

"Dana, why are you sitting over here like this girl?" When she didn't respond, Cheryl flew over to her.

"You didn't hear me calling you? What's wrong?" Cheryl kneels down and lifts her chin up so that she could see her face.

"You crying? Awe... Come here sweetheart."

In Dana's hand, was a more recent picture of LA at the Bahamas. Cheryl held the poor girl in her arms as she wailed. She'd never forgotten the sweet words LA said to her and often sat around replaying the three weeks she had fallen in love in her mind.

Diane, Jeffrey and Boo Boo all comes in. "What is it child?" Diane ask upon noticing what appeared to be tears rolling down her ebony cheeks. She saw the photo album and the picture held tightly in Dana's hand.

Jeffrey squatted next to her. "You alright Dana?"

Dana wiped away a few tears and nodded and replied, "yeah, I'm alright."

"You miss him don't you?"

Dana glanced down at the picture, "yes.... I do."

"Dana girl, you just don't know how happy you've made me. I swear, you are truly a blessing from God.

Not even a week ago, I'd given up hope. Lord have mercy.... This cute little thang right here," Diane hesitates as a tear escapes her eye. "God answered my prayers." She kisses the child's soft cheek. "God is good all the time!"

CHAPTER 50

As weeks flew by, life seemed to finally come together for Jeffrey. The kid was on a mission, working long hours on his studio album. After Jeffrey spit a couple of rhymes, Prince was hooked, even agreeing to become his manager and advising him to complete his music before opening the studio up to the public.

All this time, he never knew Jeffrey could flow so viciously. Prince hired a photographer to come and take Jeffrey's pictures for his bio. The following week, they scheduled to meet with an entertainment lawyer to sign contracts. Prince knew without a doubt that as nice as the kid was, a record deal was the least of their worries. With his flow and Prince's connects, success was imminent. Jeffrey could not believe he was finally doing what he loved... What his mom always said he had in him.

Eddie Lo had been a good friend to Jeffrey since junior high, one of the few who wasn't into crime and drugs. Both of them had sung in the same choir and written poems and music. He was the first person to come to Jeffrey's mind when Prince told him about the studio. Jeffrey messed around on the key boards, but Eddie was something like a genius. He knew everything there was to know about operating the equipment. For two weeks they worked close together, even sleeping at the studio on late nights, making major progress and headway.

Bird Park was one of the prettiest places at night. In the city, the sky was clear and the moon was bright, highlighting the scattered stars. Jeffrey and Shonda strolled through the park arm in arm, Shonda sporting a brown leather bomber with matching thigh high Steve Madden boots. She looked pretty as ever. They took a seat on a bench directly across from the water where ducks surfed and quacked all night long. Jeffrey glanced back at a police cruiser, shaking his head as it pulled up beside his ride, shining a light in and drove away. He smirked to himself as the relief of finally being legit and worry free made its impression.

Shonda suddenly breaks away from his grasp, scoots over and looks directly into his eyes. "Jeffrey, what's up with us?"

"What you mean?"

She glanced up at the sky, then back at him. "I just wanna know where we taking this thing. I mean I've been wanting this for so long, us together. I just wanna know where you at. Is your mind on me, or still on Tiffany?"

Jeffrey grins, knowing the subject would arise sooner or later. Taking in a breath of fresh air, he thought about the question.

"Damn.................. Um, Shonda I gotta keep it real with you. You know, when I was in prison, after Tiffany left me, I was fucked up. I mean, shorty broke a brotha down! I can't even front." Shonda sat there quietly as he talked. "But you know I got over that shit. By not calling or writing letters, letting her live her life, I held on by letting go, understand?"

"I think," she replied.

"I did everything I could to hold on to Tiffany and my heart got crushed, know what I'm saying?"

She nods her head. "In order for me to be at peace, I had to let go of what me and her had. I couldn't breathe." Jeffrey gazes out at the water.

"I'll always have love for her. I learned a lot. To answer your question, no. My mind ain't on getting back with Tiffany. I still think about her every now and then though. Shonda, I care for you a lot, but right now I ain't trying to rush back into another serious relationship. I'm not saying it can't happen, either. I'm just trying to get my life straight right now."

"Yeah, I feel you."

"Take it slow, be friends first alright? I wanna get to know you better, tap into that mind of yours," he said stroking her neck.

"Boy you done changed a lot. It seem like I'm talking to a totally new person."

He chuckled, "damn, is that good or bad?"

"It's good that you're maturing. Bad cause I wanna be with you like yesterday!"

"I'm just trying to build." He turned to Shonda. "You trying to build with me?"

"I'm down for whatever, just lead the way baby." Both of them broke out in laughter.

Jeffrey stared into her eyes, amazed at how attractive she was, "Anybody ever tell you how pretty you are?"

"Boy you crazy. What makes me so pretty?"

"Shorty, I'm just telling you how it is. It might sound funny cause you never had a nigga to kick it to you like this, but you're a 10 shorty in every aspect."

Shonda was absolutely stunned, speechless at how the brother was coming off at her.

'*There are no sensitive black men in the ghetto,*' she always thought. '*Just killers, dealers and fiends.*'

He embraced her tightly, shielding her snugly from a cold gust of wind.

"Jeffrey, I miss the shit out of Angie and LA. It's been two years since they died. I just can't believe..... All of these people dead, yo mama,

LA, Angie, then Black got life. Then L A's son by a girl nobody knows. And looks just like I'm too. I was mad as hell when you first told me. I felt like it should be Angie's. You ever wonder why it went down like this?"

The youngster pauses in deep thought, then comes his reply. "You know Shonda, I ain't saying we needed this shit because I'd do anything to have my mama back. But in all this drama....... In all of these deaths, I found life."

"I don't understand. What do you mean boy?"

Jeffrey turns to face Shonda, taking hold of her hands. "I guess what I'm saying is.................. **Sometimes a nigga gotta go through hell in order to find heaven.**"

CHAPTER 51

What was supposed to have been a private wedding, turned out to be an elaborate event. Once the word leaked out about the prominent couple joining hands, just about everyone they knew was trying to get an invitation. Prince knew his woman dreamed of one day getting married in front of all her friends and family. Even though he wasn't at all comfortable about being around so many strangers, he decided to go with the flow, whatever made Wanda happy.

The bachelor party was off the chain. Twenty of the prettiest strippers flew in from Atlanta to entertain Prince, his cousin Randy, Jeffrey and dozens of others were lounging in a five star suite at the Holiday Inn on West Broad Street. The elegant females showed the groom plenty of love. The thing he enjoyed the most, was chilling with the youngsters, watching them cut up with women and weed, sort of a farewell to his youthful days.

Prince decided to have the service at the same church he attended as a child. Pastor Johnny Wilkins had known his family for many years, and was delighted to wed the two. The couple could not have asked for a prettier day, a balmy Sunday in October with an occasional light breeze whisking through a cloudless sky. The place was packed with family, friends and strangers. Some of Prince's old girlfriends were among the crowd, gossiping and hating on the bride-to-be.

Britney heads the pack of flower girls as they stroll down the aisle, releasing showers of petals. Whispers could be heard from the crowd, complementing the gorgeous attire the girls had on. The Pastor quoted scriptures as bridesmaids and groomsmen formed separate lines on either side of the main isle. Jeffrey and his entourage were dressed in black tuxes by Brooks Brothers, a perfect complement to Wanders bridesmaids who were adorned in cream dresses by Betsey Johnson. Lisa, the maid of honor, walked slowly down the aisle, arm in arm with Jeffrey, then assumed her position with the other maids. Jeffrey made his way over to Reverend Wilkins, whispering briefly in his ear. The reverend nods then proceeds with the ceremony.

"Will everyone please be seated as sister Howard serenades us with her graceful voice."

The church silenced and the organ came to life as a familiar face appeared out of the woodworks, strutting down the side aisle, mike in hand. At her best, **Nikki Howard** began belting out her renown "**come share my love,**" catching the audience totally off guard as they cheered wildly for the surprise celebrity. Wanda entered the sanctuary, marching gracefully, side-by-side with her father towards the pulpit. Onlookers were captivated, confused at whether to focus their attention on **Nikki Howard** or the stunning beauty of the bride in a remarkably expensive MCM gown, an exclusive piece hand sown by Michael Cromer.

The performance came to a close as Wanda took her final step up to the altar, now the sole center of attention. Upon reaching her destination, her eyes admittedly darted frantically around the pulpit, clearly noticing the absence of her significant other! After standing bewildered for an eerily silent minute, the bride-to-be search the faces around her for an explanation as to why Prince was missing!! Wanda knew the routine of the well practiced reversal like the back of her hand, and was well aware that her man should be present by now!!!

Murmurs began to surface among the crowd as they came to realize the problem. Wanda looked up at Reverend Wilkins who returned a dumbfounded look, then turned to Shonda desperate for an answer. The proceeding had come to a screeching halt and tension mounted in the air by the second. When Shonda's eyes meet hers then dropped to the floor, so did Wanda's heart. The murmurs are now audible conversation and beads of sweat have formed all over Wanda's forehead, her palms clammy from embarrassment. Jeffrey left his post with the groomsmen and walked over to her side.

"Prince was just in his dressing chamber, said he needed some time to himself before the wedding. I told him I'll meet him in here."

Wanda glared at the youngster, closed her eyes, then whispered, **"BOY, TELL ME YOU ARE PLAYING!!!!! I got my whole family in here!!!"**

When her eyes reopened, the compassionate look on Jeffrey's face told her what she didn't want to know. **It was no game.**

"Just stay cool Wanda. I'm going to check on him right now, alright?"

Wanda said okay, but knew deep down that there was little chance the love of her life was still in the building.

Observing the best man hurry away up the aisle, Wanda's father flew over to her aid. He leaned in placing his hand on her shoulder, then whispered in a comforting tone.

"Sweetheart, this is something you have to leave up to God. Jeffrey cannot change what truly is. If your man's love is genuine, his heart will bring him down that aisle." Through the veil, he could see the agony that had built on her face as he moved closer to kiss her cheek and let her know she had his full support. He then returned to his position with the groomsmen, awaiting for the outcome.

The Ghost

CHAPTER 52

Wanda's whole world stood still. Unable to face her guests, friends and family, all she could do was continue to stare at the altar. As she did, her mind raced 100 mph and began to take over, drowning out the now audible comments echoing behind her. Wanda lowered her head as her brain attempted to answer the many unknowns. "How could Prince be late to his own wedding? Something must have happened to him. Could the reality of commitment have been too much for him and he was reconsidering?!" The last thought quickly left her mind. She knew Prince's character well and it was far from his style to get scared at the last minute.

"Why the hell would they bring me out, knowing he wasn't here?" Wanda's thoughts.

Wanda stood wallowing in a cluttered state of confusion as she contemplated the possibilities. But no matter how hard she tried to evade it, one thought lingered in her mind. It was the reason that stood out and would explain everything. As difficult as it was to come to grips with, she knew she had to face the reality of the situation.

Facing the altar, her back to all her friends and family on what was supposed to be the happiest day of her life, Wanda stood solemnly, recounting that cold and dismal day in November years back. It had taken every ounce of her courage to make the trip up to the prison that day. She started not to do it, to grab Pernell and walk into the visiting hall, smiling as usual. But in the end, her conscience prevailed, telling her there was no way she could continue to live out a fantasy, hurting the man she loved so deeply. Time had just taken its toll on their relationship. Wanda's needs had cried out for attention and her man was gone. His replacement had taken her heart, blinding her with a mere illusion of love.

Tears began to stream down the jilted brides cheek as she recounted her man's words on that fatal day.

'And in time, you'll find yourself alone. After you leave, you can never come back to me.' She searched her memory banks for any subtle hints, no matter how small, that Prince still had animosity held over from that day, but couldn't find none. Was guilt and paranoia overcoming her ability to think rationally?

A sudden roar explodes behind Wanda as the crowd erupts in a manner similar to a football stadium doing a home team touchdown. Whistles, cheers and gasps echo throughout the sanctuary, immediately snapping the bride out of her forlorn trance. When she turns around and faces the commotion, all Wanda could do is rub her eyes as they were surely deceiving her. A spectator in the audience jumped from the pew, landing on his knees in the center aisle, shouting out, "*praises to the man above, have mercy, good Lord Our Savior!!!!*"

Wanda reaches over with her right hand to touch her heart, making sure it was still beating as her knees began to wobble at the extraordinary sight....

"Hey y'all, sorry I'm late!" A powerful voice belts out from the front of the church. A wave of laughter accompanied the sound of astonishment as every eye in the building remained glued on Prince, holding a wireless microphone. Jeffrey by his side. From the reaction of the crowd, one would think he had risen out of the grave and rightfully so. By a sheer act of God, the O G was now standing tall at 6 foot 2' without so much as a cane to support him.

The organ commences to hum a quiet melody as the groom trudges down the aisle at a slow gait, best man by his side, towards the love of his life. As he walked, he lifted the microphone to his mouth.

"Sweetheart, how you doing on this lovely day?" Overcome by shock, Wanda could do nothing but stand, speechless as her father held her hand.

"It's okay baby, I know you're a little shook right now, so just listen for a moment.... Marriage is a lifelong commitment made between two people, dedicated and sharing their love and trust for its duration. Never once have I questioned the authenticity of our love. Now trust.......... It's something that's earned in time, a quality I felt I may have lost when I fell victim to that wheelchair."

"After the doctor told us there was a good possibility I would never walk again, I got scared.................. Afraid that no one, not even my Queen, could love a person in that condition." By this time, Wanda is trembling, shaking her head slowly from side to side at Prince who's now at the altar. The audience is captivated!!!!!

Utter silence reigns over the room as he reaches out to gently partake her chin in his hand. "During my lowest point in life, you stayed down and never once left my side. When I was depressed, you only encouraged me. After the therapy work started to pay off, I hid my recovery...... I guess you could say it was........ A test of your dedication, and I apologize for ever doubting your faith. But baby, during this struggle, you did more than prove yourself to me. You gave me reassurance that our love is unconditional, for better or worse, and that my love is priceless. Wanda, on a scale of 1 to 10, you a 12 baby. Real talk, you possess all the qualities I need in a woman and then some. I wouldn't trade you in for the world." Prince inches forward and embraces her tightly by her waist. "So what's up sweetie, you ready to be Mrs. Miller?"

Wanda throws her arms around her man, clinging on for dear life, then she speaks through a tearful sob,

"*Y- YESSSS........... Lord knows I am Prince!!!!*"

The crowd goes wild as the two interlock for what seemed to be an eternity. After several waves of applause and outcries from on lookers, the couple finally let go of one another as the Reverend prompted them to recite their vows. Many *ooh's* and *ahh's* filled the air as audience members gawked at the size of the diamond boulder Prince slipped on Wanda's finger.

"I now pronounce you husband and wife... You may kiss the bride!"

It was final. The couple expressed their love, basking in matrimony while the crowd went berserk. Outside, the bride took off her cummerbund and tossed it backwards into the crowd of bridesmaids. Everyone watched to see who would be next in line to be married. When Shonda emerged from the bunch, waving it proudly, the crowd erupted into a frenzy.

"Well I'll be damn," Jeffrey says under his breath to Eco as they wait by the stretch limo. The guess as they were leaving, shouted "CONGRAT-ULATIONS," to the newlyweds as they pulled off with a convoy of limos in tow.

CHAPTER 53

The reception had an enormous turnout, held in the same hotel where Prince proposed. Scores of big boy hustlers around the city even drop by to congratulate the ghetto superstar and his new bride. Even *crack head* Geraldine attended, quickly making her way to the dance floor to get her grove on. The place was swarming with folks, happily indulging themselves in the exquisite food and drinks.

The married couple was seated in a secluded table for two in the far corner. It was a momentous occasion for Jeffrey as he sat at a huge round table in the center of the ball room, sipping Premium bubbly with all of his close friends.

"This shit here is the life!" Jeffrey says and raise his bottle. Prince hold up a bottle of Moet in salute. The O G returns the gesture as he nods his head. Erica and Shonda walks over with a camera and began snapping photos of everyone at Jeffrey's table. The liquor takes an effect as the youngster stands, clowning while striking poses for the camera. His boys follow suit and has the entire reception in laughs.

Prince strained his eyes at the beautiful female standing out in the crowd, looking lost. She was adorned in Muslim garments, giving her a distinctive appearance. After a few minutes of searching through the crowd of faces, the two catch each other's eye and the uniquely dressed woman makes her way over towards the table. Prince takes a sip from his champagne glass and places it down on the table as he greet Sister Pearl Muhammad.

"How you doing? I was hoping you was gonna make it. Wanda this is Pearl, Justice's wife. Pearl, this is my beautiful wife Wanda."

After the women exchange pleasantries, Pearl hugs the O G.

"You know I wouldn't miss your wedding for the world. You are full of surprises. Look at you. Walking.... **WOW ..... God is great isn't He**?"

"Yes, He is," Prince agrees.

"Congratulations to you both."

"Thank you.... Can I get you anything Mrs. Pearl?" Asked Wanda.

"Call me Pearl. But No thanks, I appreciate it though." Pearl turns to Prince, "the brother sends his regards."

"How is he?"

"Holding strong, all praises due to Allah."

"Good good."

"Be right back sweetie, nice meeting you Pearl." Wanda kisses her husband, then rushes over to greet her mother who just arrived.

"So what's up sis? He need anything?"

Pearl smiles. "He's alright. I went to see him last week. I tried to catch you at the church to give you something." She glanced around at all the young people drinking.

"You know this is not my type of party." Prince laughs as Pearl pulls two envelopes from her pocketbook.

"This is yours, this one is for Jeffrey." She stands up, "I have to get back to the temple."

"Sister at least let me introduce you to Jeffrey before you leave. He's right over there. He's a good kid." Before she could object, Prince waves

Jeffrey over. The youngster quickly straighten himself up as he approaches the stranger.

"Jeffrey, I want you to meet a very good friend of mine. This here is Pearl, Kihiem's wife. This is Jeffrey."

Sister Pearl Muhammad was a goddess and her very presence demanded respect. "It's a pleasure to meet you sister. I've heard a lot about you."

"You too brother Jeffrey." The three sat there, chatting for a few minutes, then Pearl explains that she's running late and needed to return to the Mosque.

"Well, I'm sorry I can't stay longer." Pearl tells Prince. "Take care now. See you later Jeffrey." Pearl turns and walks away. Jeffrey watches her in awe until she disappears through the door. She was absolutely beautiful.

When he turns back around, Prince hands him an envelope. "From your brother Kihiem."

"Oh yeah?" Jeffrey takes the letter, stare at it as if he was trying to read through the envelope, then sat down next to Prince.

"As crazy as it may sound, I know I should hate him for what he did......... But I don't and I don't know why."

"Because you are maturing...... None of our hands are clean Jeffrey. Think about your life and the people you've hurt. Are you and I any better than Justice?" Prince pauses for a moment in deep thought. "This street shit is a bitch and if you're in it, sometimes you gotta get lower than the beast himself to hold what you have together."

"I certainly feel that. You right mane. I think about all my niggas and just that whole shit with LA, was straight unreal. That shit could be a book or a movie for real. All those killings behind what? I've done some of the wildest shit out here in these streets to survive. So I can relate to living lower than a beast. After my mama died, I ain't give a fuck!!!"

"And now...." Prince was testing the kid.

"Mane now... Thanks to God and you, I can really focus on what I need to be doing with the rest of my life. I'm grateful for a second chance at life because I've done shit that could have sent me away forever."

Flashback (**BOOM!!!BOOM!!! BOOM!!!!**) Gunshots and the guy who'd robbed him drops to the ground.)
Jeffrey shakes his head and tries to rid himself of such thoughts. He catches Prince staring at him.

"What?" Jeffrey asked.

"Prince looks him in the eyes. "You made now playa."

"Made..................... What you mean?"

"You got *money, attitude, dedication and hella education*. You *M.A.D.E* youngster." They sat, laughing and reminiscing about the past. Hours fly by and the party has come to an end. Before leaving, Jeffrey dips off to an area where no one else is at and opens the envelope Prince gave to him. The letter reads as follows.

Dear Brotha Jeffrey,

I was delighted to receive your thoughts. First, I would like to apologize for not coming clean with you while you were here. I tried man believe me. I just couldn't do it. When I read your letter, I could feel the strength in your words. Thanks man, I did not know how you would feel about me after you found out. You have grown up a lot in a short time. I miss you brother and I'm happy that things are going well for you and your family. Stay focused out there. When you get to the top, keep your relay hand behind you so you can pull another brother with you and pass on some of that knowledge. This letter is very brief but that's only because I know you're a busy man. Peace Jeffrey and may Allah bless you with much success!

Your friend and brother Kihiem Muhammad

"My brother," Jeffrey smiles and places the letter back inside the envelope.

"Erica, Britney, are y'all ready?" They were still at the table with

Prince and Wanda. "Ya'll ready?" He asked again.

"Yup," replied Erica. Britney jumps up and hugs Wanda then Prince. "You be easy playa," Prince says giving Jeffrey dap.

"Call me before you leave for the honeymoon. We gone kick back at the crib man. Congratulations," Jeffrey says again, bear hugging his mentor.

"Thanks Prince," he whispers to the O G. Shonda scoops Brittney into her arms then takes hold of Jeffrey's hand.

"Bye everyone," Erica yells as the four heads to the elevator. Prince couldn't help but smile at the loving family as they departed.

The ride back from the hotel was quiet. Britney had fallen asleep in the backseat. Jeffrey glanced over at Erica, watching her nod off as well. As he drives slowly past the cemetery where his mother was laid to rest, realizing there was no traffic, he bucks a quick u-turn.

The cemetery was empty as Jeffrey pulled in. He and Shonda quietly slipped out of the car, trying not to wake his sisters. The two walked 20 yards or so before they arrived in front of Joanne's tombstone. Shonda picked off the wilted flowers and tossed them to the side as Jeffrey knelt down beside the grave, not caring about his new tuxedo. He took a deep breath, then stared around at all the other tombstones. Shonda knelt down, embracing him from behind as he cleared his throat.

"Mama....," He hesitates. "It's been one hella trip. I think about all the things you used to tell me. You said the streets was nothing. I remember how you would say drugs destroyed our people. You was right. Every

235

time I hurt, every time I've cried or felt pain, the streets was always some how responsible. I guess it won't meant for me to fall victim out here. Every day is a blessing. I could've been dead a long time ago, but for some reason, God saw something in me that I didn't see in myself.

I see now. I can hear now. No longer are my eyes closed to the harsh realities of life. We love you mama. I wish you could be here. When I think back on everything we've been through, it still hurts at times. But we continue to strive. We gone hold you down, so you rest in peace, okay? I suppose losing you was all part of my tribulation. For the first time in a long time, I'm happy. It's been a long time coming..." He pauses as Erica and Britney comes walking up. He takes each sister's hand as they comes to stand on each side of him.

"We back together mama and nothing but death will separate us again." Jeffrey gaze up at the remarkable skyline and smile.

"The strife is over... Battle is done... I'm free at last... Thank God, I'm free at last!!!!"

THEE END

A GHOST TALE

A word from the Author

When I first started to write this novel, I had war on my mind, anger in my heart and hatred for my own kind. This life of mine has truly been a rough journey but through it all, I've learned something important. And that is, war can't give life, it can only take it away. We are killing each other because we don't know one another. We have no sense of who we are or where we come from. Therefore, we are lost in this life, stumbling with no direction.

Brothers, we must stop the killing! Please believe that I feel your struggle. I am very conscious of my history and the suffering that my people had to endure for centuries just so future generations could have a chance at life, liberty and equality....... But ask yourselves, are we living or are we dying every day in the streets at an all time rate? Is there liberty or are we still confined in captivity all across this country, filling the prisons and cemeteries by the minute? Is there equality for our people? I think not. So what did our ancestors really die for?

As we began to grasp the concept of unification and educate our children, we'll start to see murders decrease. Over the years, I have developed a special kind of love for my people and every time one of you are murdered in the streets, I feel a part of me being ripped away. My heart aches when thinking about the pain we inflict on each other. I flow from deep within, **no ink**, only blood, sweat and tears coming from my pen, speaking to all my brothers and sisters who are misunderstood. Who needs someone to tell them the truth and shed some light over the darkness.

Before I close, I would like to say a brief word to my elders who read this novel. Give the youngsters a chance. Our own people give up on us. You have so much wisdom to pass down. Let's come together. We need you and you need us to carry on your legacy.... **If you don't believe in us, then who will?**

"Ghost"

FICTIONS BEST KEPT SECRET... THE GHOST

Other published books by the Author,
Cold Blooded: The New Year's Day Massacre (**True Story**)
Tribulation Of A Ghetto Kid, The Street Bible... The Trilogy.
Mass Appeal and its explosive sequel, **The Thril**l.
FIRE BUG
Black Girl Found

Made in the USA
Middletown, DE
04 August 2020